IN SEARCH OF THE PERFECT LOVER AND FINDING YOURSELF INSTEAD!

ELAINE: An old hand at leaving men, an Army commando when it came to the battle of the sexes—her wisecracks masked an inability to get close and find fulfillment with anyone.

JEANNETTE: She dropped a bombshell on the group when she announced her passionate affair with a 19-year-old actor. If she were a 34-year-old man, people would call it virility. Elaine wants to know, "Do you screw him or adopt him?"

SUE: Of the dullest marriage imaginable—hasn't made love for six months—at least not with her husband. Maybe that's why she can't keep her hands off other men.

ERICA: The only one with a stable relationship—until her husband shacks up with a 26-year-old he met in Bloomingdale's, and suddenly, for Erica, it's one night stands or learning to be oneself with someone else.

an unmarried woman

A NOVEL BY
Carol DeChellis Hill

BASED ON A SCREENPLAY BY
Paul Mazursky

AVON
PUBLISHERS OF BARD, CAMELOT AND DISCUS BOOKS

AN UNMARRIED WOMAN is an original publication of Avon Books. This work has never before appeared in book form.

Cover Design: Artwork Title Copyright © 1977 by Twentieth Century Fox

AVON BOOKS
A division of
The Hearst Corporation
959 Eighth Avenue
New York, New York 10019

Published by arrangement with Paul Mazursky.
Library of Congress Catalog Card Number: 77-93539
ISBN: 0-380-01834-9

First Avon Printing, February, 1978

Printed in Canada

an unmarried woman

1

IT WAS a New York day. That was what Martin would have called it. Sky high with dog shit. Erica smiled as she thought of him stuck that morning as they jogged around the park. Dog shit. Martin hated dog shit more than anything. Even Republicans. Erica wiped the sole of her boot in one deft stroke against the curb and it was gone. She spun around and paid the taxi driver through the window, a new habit she rather liked, noted his appraising glance at her in her dark green slacks, her fox jacket and hat, noted, and liked the fact that she did have one hell of a terrific ass. With a good ass, a smart head, a pretty face, and a husband she adored, what more could a woman want?

Erica didn't ask herself that question. But her friends did. They asked her and asked her and asked her. Erica, what do you want? I don't want anything, Erica would shrug, and smile, and then laugh. They hated that. "You're so self-satisfied," Elaine would say, in her dark, prodding way. Elaine said it like it was like a joke, only not quite. Elaine would have preferred to hate Erica, but Erica knew that in fact Elaine loved Erica, loved the idea of Erica, Erica with the perfect life, the Erica who was sometimes too much for her friends. When Erica sat back against the bony back of the cane chairs in Maxwell's Plum and regarded her friends, she saw a good-looking, middle-thirties group; all without men. Without permanent men. Except Erica.

Erica of the perfect husband, perfect fifteen-year-old daughter, and perhaps the most relentless target of the jealousy, Erica of the perfect ass.

The perfect, beautiful, magnificent Erica was about to go through the worst crisis of her life. They did not know this, Erica did not know this, nor even did the perfect husband know this, at least not fully. For that November morning, he and Erica had gone to the park and jogged as usual. They had made love as usual afterward. Erica had lain in his arms, as usual; afterward they had smoked cigarettes and murmured and then, slowly, languidly, in the languid morning manner of the upper middle class self-employed, had gotten dressed. Slowly, languidly, with great affection, and something. Something else. Erica felt it so timorously on the edge of her mind, such a faint sparkle of something hidden, she let it slip past, slip past her with the sound and hiss of the silk chemise going over her head, a whisper of recognition that went unrecognized.

It was Martin. He looked peculiar.

"Are you all right?" she said.

"Yeah, yeah," he said.

"Why do you look like that?"

"I'm thinking."

"What are you thinking?"

"I'm thinking that you have a terrific ass." He smiled at her.

"Well, if it's so good, what is so bad?"

"I have my checkup at the doctor's today."

"So?"

"So you know how I worry about it."

"Worry about it? Are you worried you have something, you mean? I mean, nobody worries about a checkup. They worry if they have something the checkup might make it come true, if that's what you mean. I mean, are you worried, Martin?" She walked over to him, concerned.

"Well, men of my age, you know, you never know."

"You never know what?"

"Well, hearts, their minds, you know, it's the age when a lot of men feel tired. They go off to Tahiti and start weaving mats."

"You want to weave mats?" Erica said, smiling.

"When I feel tired I think about it."

"Well, keep thinking about it. In fact, I'd even give it a try. I give you three hours with mat making. Tops." She pulled on her boots, snapped her bracelet in place, and brushed his cheek with her lips. "I don't hear Patti. She must have run off to school without even a good-bye."

When Erica went down the stairs to make breakfast, her eye caught the note Patti had left on the table. "Did the earth move? Love, Patti." Erica snatched up the note and smiled. She was much too precocious for a fifteen-year-old. "Well, what do you think I think when the door is locked?" Patti had said to her. "Of course I know you're making love." That was one of the few times in her life Erica had blushed.

She went into the kitchen, put on the coffee, set the table, and got the paper in from the door. She put some muffins in to warm in the toaster oven and sat down with the paper for a few minutes alone, before Martin arrived. She would always be the first dressed, the first anything. She was quick, that was all, but Martin had once wisely said to her, "It's not that you're quick, it's that you cannot bear transitions. You just pass from moment to moment as quickly as possible so you don't have to note that that is what you are doing." Erica knew he was right, but it was so unlike him to express that kind of observation, and she was so stung by it, by the truth of it, that she had to ignore it.

"Are you making my favorite eggs?" Martin called down to her.

"O.K." She didn't really feel like it, but that meant

that the sex had been terrific. Martin always wanted eggs with hot sauce and grated cheese after the sex had been sublime. She was surprised in that it had been good but not, she thought, sublime. Actually she suspected she reserved sublimity for her truly intoxicated or stoned moments. She didn't like to drink, but she loved those moments when she did get drunk, seldom enough, when her mind spun out of control, when words, phrases burst from her mouth that shocked her, surprised her, and the lovemaking then seemed very dreamlike, as if it couldn't be happening to her, but it was happening to her, only it wasn't really her because she was drunk. It had occurred to her more than once that there was something to the fact that her most intense moments occurred when she was able to say it wasn't really her. That thought, too, disturbed her.

Before Martin left that morning, he grabbed Erica and kissed her in such a passionate way it left her stunned.

"You're only going for a checkup," she said, "you're not going to die."

Martin's face was tight. He nodded. "Right."

"Right," she said, and closed the door. What was the matter with men that they thought every physical assault was a matter of life and death? A six-foot, healthy forty-five-year-old man who thought every evidence of a cold was the first sign of pneumonia. She laughed, with affection, at Martin's preoccupation, and began to clear the dishes. As she moved the dishes from the table to the kitchen sink, that faint, strange feeling assailed her again. Like a melody not quite heard, but heard subliminally, she felt some disturbance, something. And then she shrugged it off. Or tried to. Briefly she felt very cold. Something in Martin's kiss had made her cold. Stone cold. Maybe I should call Arthur Jacobs, she thought. And be embarrassed again? Totally embarrassed again? Erica remembered the scene last summer in Dr. Jacobs's office. Absurd was all that Erica could think of at the time. It had been so absurd. Absurd. Absurd beyond belief absurd. She had sat there, composed, cheerful Erica, and after the examination Dr. Jacobs had said, "Erica, organically there's nothing wrong with you. I can't explain your appetite difficulty."

It had been odd. Erica had suddenly, in the middle of the summer, found herself losing weight, losing weight inexorably. She had been blessed with a rare and totally predictable metabolism, always always five feet six, always always 125. Then 120, then 118, then 113. People said she looked good, but something in it disturbed her.

"Can you describe your symptoms?" Dr. Jacobs had asked.

"Well, it's like," Erica said, "it's like it's stop go, stop go. I mean, I feel hungry, and then the minute the food gets in my mouth, I change my mind. I'm not hungry at all. It has nothing to do with my taste. It's just that I can't seem to make up my mind whether I want to swallow it or not. I just can't get past that moment. Sometimes I fool around with this back and forth for fifteen minutes. It's driving Martin crazy."

"Are you emotionally upset about anything?"

"No, Arthur," Erica had said, "there is absolutely nothing. I have a good family life, I—" and then, startlingly, surprisingly, and humiliatingly, her voice broke, a catch occurred, and tears started to slip down her cheeks. "I, I don't know what it is. I, I feel upset, I feel upset, I don't know why," and she had sobbed then, her hands hiding her face.

When she recovered, she composed herself, apologized for the outburst, and said it often occurred during her menstrual period. The doctor, equally relieved at some clarification, had smiled and said, "I understand," had slipped some pills into her hand and said, "These will relieve your symptoms. Stomach relaxant."

After that, Erica had taken a long walk down Fifth Avenue. She thought, and heard herself say again and again, "There's nothing wrong with my life, it's just me. Just me. Dissatisfied. Something." She had said this once to Elaine, who had turned on her viciously and said, "You never have any right for even a moment's unhappiness. For chrissake, Erica, everybody gets a down day now and then. As perfect as everything is, nothing ever really is." But Jeannette, wiser, sadder, had said, "That's what we all say, 'There's nothing really wrong, it's just me. I don't fit. I'm the one who's petulant, the world's all right, but I'm all wrong.' Well, if that's what we think, we ought to unthink it. It stinks. That's really woman shit."

Erica had been amazed. But out of that had come the agreement to meet once a week, in bars, for drinks, the "group" that really was a consciousness-raising group. But they couldn't bear to call it that, somehow. They couldn't quite bear it to be that. They couldn't finally trust each other enough to tell the whole truth. But they told enough.

After two or three weeks of those meetings, Erica had felt perfectly fine. By comparison, her life was incredible. The desperate song being sung every week was, "Everything's fine, but I have no man." Erica wondered sometimes at the expression, "No man. I need a man." The *idea* of a man, not I need someone to love me, but I need a Man in my life. She didn't think men thought of women like that, as some final guarantee against insignificance, some proof of existence. It had come to her as a shock that that was really what they were all saying, as if, "When I have a man, then life will be really real. I will be real. I will be worthy." It was not, "When I have a man to love, we can love each other and that will be rich." No. It was not that. It made Erica wonder if she were that dependent on Martin. She didn't think so. But increasingly she wondered how much she knew her own mind.

And then this morning, the coldness again. The pills had cured the swallow-or-not-to-swallow business, but somehow she had not cured the chills. That had been the other symptom. A coldness. Even in the summer.

"Probably the air conditioning. Wear a sweater," Dr. Arthur Jacobs had said, putting his hand on Erica's shoulder. Even as he said it, Erica had felt better.

Erica carefully washed out a cup. She wanted to wash the dishes. No dishwasher this morning. She wanted to feel the round smoothness inside the cup, rinse it up out of the suds, shining and clean. She could be a real housefrau if she ever let it go. The sun poured in through the kitchen window then, and she forgot the chill.

When she finished washing the breakfast things, she called the gallery and told them she'd be a few minutes late. The virtues of a part-time job. The Rowan Gallery in SoHo was definitely a downtown gallery, but quickly becoming the hub of the new New York talent. Several uptown galleries were beginning to get the drift, and one had even moved its offices downtown, where the artists were. Prices being what they were, Herb Rowan, Erica's boss, said all the artists were moving further south down into Chinatown. "It fits," he had said, "there's a close affinity between abstract expressionism and egg foo yung."

"If Saul ever heard you say that, he'd kill you," Erica said.

"He knows I don't mean it," Herb said. "Would I tear down my own bread and butter?"

"*You* might," Erica said, smiling. "I think you're jealous."

"Jealous," Herb had grumbled. "Jealous. Jealous of these idiots who come in here speckling red and yellow paint over a canvas and walk out with a couple thousand dollars? What's it take 'em? A couple hours, and that's all, a lotta chutzpah. I sell it, I do all the work, I line up the suckers, and what do I get, a lousy twenty percent."

"That's outrageous," Erica said.

"What do you mean outrageous? You know what the markup in retail is? Two hundred percent, that's what," Herb would go on, mumbling like a merchant who wanted nothing more than to bilk either the wholesaler or the public. Erica knew it was sheer bluff. There was the merchant side, and it was greedy, but the stronger side was Herb's own fascination with art, and with the artists; with, Erica thought, the mysterious process of creation, so outside Herb's own ability, so central to his ambition. Herb's paintings hung in his office. No one ever said anything about them. They had hung there year after year. The first year she worked at the gallery, Erica, in a soft moment, told Herb she wanted to buy one. He sensed her condescension and embarrassed her by saying gruffly, "You couldn't afford it. My prices are too high." And so she never mentioned it again, and he arranged the paintings so they now hung with their price tags proudly displayed: $40,000, $65,000, and one small canvas for $20,000. The prices were comparable with the most expensive artists in the gallery.

When Erica arrived at the gallery, Charlie Todd was there. Charlie had an immense amount of talent, sold well, and was crusted with such machismo that Erica often found she didn't like him.

"Hi, Erica," he said, "looking very good, considering your age."

"How aged do you think I am?"

"You must be close to forty, with a fifteen-year-old daughter."

"Wrong again, Charlie. I was married early. I'm thirty-six."

"You're only thirty-six?" he said, the perpetual blade of grass, the total city affectation, hanging from his lips, the brooding but amused glance, the Mexican Apache sweater. "Then I take it back. You don't look so good."

"Thanks, Charlie." Erica went to the back of the gallery and pulled out some of Saul Kaplan's paintings. She had promised him she would have them hung by this afternoon so he could check and recheck. She liked Kaplan. He was one of the best artists in New York City, and seemed totally unconcerned with his reputation. And he was handsome, in a sort of lumberjack way, but with none of Charlie's pretentious machismo.

As she bent over, Charlie stroked her ass.

"Find some new canvas, Charlie," she said, standing up.

Charlie smiled. "The trouble with you, Erica, is you think you're fooling people. But you don't fool me. I can always tell what a woman is feeling by her eyes."

"Can't you tell what a man is feeling by his eyes?"

"It's not the same. I can tell, Erica, you are leading a very sheltered life." He moved his face closer to her. "But most important of all, I can tell you you're not getting enough."

"Charlie," Erica said, moving toward him, "I think you better have your eyes examined."

"It's true, isn't it? You aren't getting enough?"

"Charlie, I am getting so much I have to have iron injections every day in order to walk around. That's how bad it is."

She moved the canvas out into the main gallery.

"That's Kaplan's latest. He having a show?"

"Yes. He's really good, isn't he?"

Charlie shrugged. "If you like it."

"Charlie, come on!" Erica was amazed at such an absence of generosity. "You're good, Charlie," she said, she couldn't resist. "You could give Saul a break and say he's good."

"Maybe I don't think he's good," Charlie said.

"Maybe you think he's better," Erica said.

"He's not better!" Charlie screamed at her, and slammed out of the gallery.

"Life after high school," Erica murmured, "there really isn't any."

Herb came out of the back. "Where's Charlie?"

"He left. I insulted him."

"Why?"

"I got angry, I guess. I thought creative people had sensitivity. Charlie has zero."

"Sometimes," Herb shrugged, "God makes mistakes." The phone rang and Herb picked it up. "It's for you. Personal. On my time."

Erica breezed past him. "You always were a generous man." She picked up the phone. It was Elaine. "Look, I want to be sure you're coming tonight."

"Of course I'm coming tonight. Have I ever missed a meeting?"

"Yes. That's why I'm calling you."

"Something special happening tonight?"

"Yes."

"What?"

"I can't tell you."

"Why not?"

"It's Jeannette's news. She'd kill me."

"I bet you're going to tell me."

"She has a man."

"Jeannette?"

"Believe it or not."

"Tell me. He's married?"

"Worse."

"Elaine!"

"He's queer."

"Worse."

"I'm hanging up. Good-bye."

Erica smiled as she put down the receiver. How typical of Elaine. "I'm hanging up." She always announced it before she did it. "I'm leaving now. I'm saying goodbye"—all those announcements. Erica felt for a moment a strong bond of affection for Elaine. She sighed. "If only she weren't so damn complicated, I might even be able to love her." But then again, she thought, probably not. She thought feeling love for a woman was a very difficult thing. Loving a man was easy. Natural. For whatever reasons of tuning, of instinct, of habit, practice, she trusted men in a way she could never trust women. Erica felt that, deep down, in these meetings with her friends, that the envy they felt of her marriage drove them apart. She had always felt that they would all run after Martin in a minute if she allowed it. She had confessed this once jokingly to Elaine, who said simply, "Not all of them. I'm the only one who's sexually attracted to Martin." Elaine was capable of that. Elaine.

Elaine, who had called Erica after she had walked out on Steven, husband number two, over three years ago, had walked out on handsome, gorgeous, and yet somehow pathetic Steven, and called Erica to declare she had.

"I don't understand why you walked out." That's all Erica had said. "I can't be the only one who's surprised."

"No, everybody's so surprised I'm disgusted with myself," Elaine said. "I must really put on a good act."

"You liked Steven a lot, Elaine. It wasn't an act."

"Yes," she said.

Erica thought she sounded sad.

"I liked him, but I didn't want to, I really don't want to be really close to anybody. It's the truth, Erica. I start to suffocate. I think I'm going to die. The more he loved me, the more he killed me." Her voice broke. "I have to be far enough away to feel close, but not so close to feel hurt. It's called the perfect balance, that's what makes me happy. There's only one problem with that"—Elaine laughed almost hysterically through the tears now—"It doesn't exist." Then her voice changed to a plaintive tone.

"Look, he's upset. He might, you know, call you." Erica heard the tension in her voice.

"Well, so he calls me. Anything special you want me to say, or not to say?"

"Well, he'll probably ask you to lunch," Elaine said, her voice catching.

"Yes?" Erica said.

"You won't go, will you?" Elaine said, pleading. Erica was somehow so pulled, so torn by that request. Frankly and honestly, Erica thought Steven Belknap one of the most handsome, and unqualifiedly, absolutely, the most boring man on the face of the earth. Lunch would have been an eternity, and she would have finessed it into a drink, or coffee. Elaine, though, so seduced by Steven, so seduced, Erica suspected, she almost had to leave him because he overwhelmed her so, now Elaine was afraid, afraid Erica would take the prize away.

"Elaine, for God's sake, I'm not going to make a pass at Steven."

"He will at you, though," she said bitterly, "he thinks you're terrific."

"Elaine, I think we better talk. You sound a wreck. You want to come over?"

"No, I want to go to a gay bar."

"Why?" Erica laughed.

"I want to go somewhere where no one makes a pass at you, so I don't feel inadequate."

So they had. Absurdly crept into a crowded gay bar in the Village, absurdly sat at a table, politely, coldly tolerated while Elaine spilled out the story that she knew deep down how attracted Steven was to Erica, that she had to leave him because he suffocated her, and she was the logical next woman.

Erica had said, not gently enough, "Elaine, I don't think Steven has the hots for me. I think you do." And Elaine, face burning, had said, "Not a chance. I hate you too much."

"Thanks," Erica had said. "Well, Steve doesn't want me, so forget it."

"How do you know?"

"Give me credit for something," Erica snapped. "And even if he did? I don't want anyone, can't you get that?"

"You keep on saying that. I can't believe it. Never wanted any guy but Martin? Not ever?"

"Passing fancies, you know," Erica shrugged, "tennis instructors, ski instructors, I have kind of an instructor thing. But never where I really wanted to, you know, go through with anything."

"Ever kissed another man?"

Erica laughed. "No. If I was going to fool around, I'd at least fool around. Let's go."

Erica left the gallery early to get some shopping done before she met the "group" tonight, and decided to stop home first. As she opened the door, she heard sounds, giggling upstairs, and, walking into the house, knew it was Patti and Phil. She was embarrassed. Should she stop them? After all, they were in her house and she didn't like it. She knocked on Patti's door.

"Patti."

"I'm busy."

"Unlock this door," Erica snapped.

"In a minute."

She could hear scuffling inside. "What's going on?" Erica demanded. "Patti, open this door." She was amazed at her own desperation. "Patti!"

The door opened. Phil stood there, flushed and sheepish. Patti, pink and proud.

"What is it? Don't get hysterical. We were only necking."

"I don't like necking behind closed doors," Erica said, shaking.

"We didn't want to be interrupted," Patti said, smiling.

"Well, you can't neck here," Erica said. She didn't quite know what to do.

"Look, I'm practically the only virgin in my class," Patti said, raising a hand, "by choice, by choice. I mean, I know how to take care of myself."

"I'd still feel better if you went downstairs. And don't neck in the house."

"You want me to neck in the car?"

"That's better."

"O.K. Come on, Phil, let's go out to the car."

"I think your sense of timing needs improvement."

"What do you want, Mom?"

"I want you to want a piece of cake and a glass of milk."

"You have any?" Patti said, smiling.

Erica sighed, "Yes," and went and got it. At fifteen, Patti had more composure, Erica thought, than she would ever have in her life. Composure and rebellion, she thought. Either an envious combination or a self-contradicting one.

Erica, Phil, and Patti left the house together, Erica feeling like some old war-horse, some noble beast that had made its best efforts in a time gone by. She felt so out of tune with this generation. What was it? She wasn't hung up—at least she didn't think so—but God, they made her feel that way. You had to set some rules, didn't you?

Patti had said to her, "Do you think sex is dirty?"

"No, of course not," Erica had replied, surprised.

"Then why do you think it's dirty for me?"

"I don't think it's dirty," Erica had said, "I just don't think you're at an age when you can handle it."

"I wonder if that's really the reason," Patti had said, and Erica had said nothing.

Erica's taxi arrived at P. J. Clarke's a little after nine. She was an hour late. She had spent that hour walking, thinking, dreaming around Fifth Avenue, bundled up in the cold, enjoying the privacy of being totally alone, wondering if she would ever get the time or the impulse to paint again, wondering why Martin hadn't called her, she had to call him to find out about the checkup, wondering about the strained sound in his voice, wondering.

Erica walked into the crowded bar. She moved past the singles line, rows of attractive men—dressed, she felt, for the hunt. They looked her over carefully, the polished hair, the makeup—Erica could look great when she tried—the fox jacket, the Cacharel pants, Bendel boots. Erica knew she looked—and liked the moment—the total New York Girl. Several of the men's eyes met hers, held, and she moved on. The rest of the women were seated at a table, talking animatedly, and seeing Erica, Jeannette jumped up, "At last, now for the story of the evening!" Erica kissed Sue on the cheek, embraced Jeannette, and sat down. "You must tell me right away, the suspense is killing me."

"It couldn't have killed you too much, you're an hour late," Elaine said.

Erica ordered a beer and sat back, noting the light in Jeannette's face.

"O.K., are you ready?"

"We're ready," they chorused.

"I met a man," Jeannette said faintly. For reasons beyond them, they all burst into gales of laughter.

Tables turned. Jeannette whispered, "I'm serious." They were quiet.

"The problem is," she said—here it comes, Erica thought—"he's very young."

"Young?" Erica said. Somehow that was the last problem she would have imagined. "Well, how young?"

Jeannette hesitated, gluing her eyes to their faces, not wanting to miss a flicker of response, "He's nineteen."

"My God," Erica said.

"Nineteen?" Sue said, squeaking out her bewilderment.

"But he's very mature," Jeannette said. "He's unbelievable."

"Does he know how to do it yet?" Elaine said.

"Oh, Elaine," Jeannette blushed, "for the first time. I came."

"Oh, my God. Another beer." Elaine jumped up and hugged Jeannette. Erica was embarrassed. It was like winning first prize in the horse show.

"Well, if he's good in bed, there's only one question left to resolve," Elaine said.

"What?" Jeannette said.

"Do you fuck him, or do you adopt him?" Elaine burst into her hearty laugh. It rang, pealing off the walls, making heads at the next table turn. Despite herself, Erica laughed. Elaine enjoying her own outrageous humor was hilarious in itself. And nineteen—somehow that *was* funny. But Erica knew Jeannette was serious.

"I don't want to be his mother," Jeannette said very seriously.

"Why not?" Elaine snapped. "A good kid is hard to find."

"I think you're going through early menopause," Sue said. "You could never be this mean otherwise."

"Mean? You think this is mean? This is my kind phase," Elaine said. "Look, you don't like me anymore, I'm a little drunk, and I'm going to the can."

Erica turned to Jeannette. "Tell me about him."

"He's an actor."

"Does he work?"

"Yes. He understudied Romeo in that Shakespeare-in-the-Park last summer. Is that ironic? I mean, I've dated so many men, and Steve—his name is Steve—well, he's so mature. He's the first man I've liked since my divorce. He's different. He's not afraid to be tender. No games. He doesn't come on. Oh, I don't know. I am in love with him. Am I crazy?"

"No more than anybody else," Erica said. "I suppose if you were a thirty-four-year-old guy and you met a nineteen-year-old girl, nobody would think twice about it. They'd think it was virile of you."

"He wants to live with me," Jeannette said.

"So soon?" Erica said.

"It's been three months," Jeannette said.

"Oh." Erica wondered then how honest they all were capable of being with each other.

"I mean, I've said things to him I've never said to anyone. Real things. Really me things. And the sex. I never really knew what it was before."

Elaine came swaggering back and couldn't resist, "I knew you didn't the minute you told me kissing was better." They all burst into laughter.

"I have to tell you something." Jeannette looked around almost conspiratorially. "Promise you won't laugh?"

"We won't," Erica smiled.

"Well, last night he undressed me. Then he gave me the most incredible massage I've ever had."

"Was it sexual?" Erica said.

"Well, it was and it wasn't. He massaged my toes, and my fingers, and my eyes. He actually massaged my eyes. Then he massaged me, my sex, and I had an orgasm and then another and another." She leaned back, closing her eyes.

"I think it was sexual," Elaine said.

"God," Sue said, "I haven't had one of those good old-fashioned clitoral orgasms in years. What is this boy's number?"

Jeannette was quiet. "What should I do?"

"Jeannette," Erica said, "don't be offended. But are you sure he's being honest with you? I mean, how serious can a nineteen-year-old man be?"

"Boy, is that naive, Erica."

"What's naive about it?"

"What man is honest?" Elaine said. "They can't be honest. It's all wrapped up in sexual ego."

"What the hell is sexual ego?" Sue said.

"Never getting enough. Always on the make, performance-oriented. In any event, sex-oriented."

"Oh," Sue said, waving a nonchalant hand, "there are plenty of men who are interested in more than sex."

"Name one," Elaine said.

"My husband. He hasn't balled me in six months." She laughed then, in a way that startled them. They didn't know whether to believe her or not. They decided to ignore it. Erica somehow noticed that Sue had been drinking a lot lately. She worried, but wanted to forget it.

"I adore you, Elaine," Erica said, "but I really think you're getting to be a man-hater."

"I love men," Elaine said, "I just think they're not honest. Do you think Martin is being totally honest with you?"

"I don't think about it."

"Maybe he's having an affair."

"I know he's not having an affair."

"How do you know?"

"Because I know. Some things you know. What you know, you know, that's all. Besides, he's always hot. He's hotter the last year than ever. He's forty-five years old, Elaine. He'd be dead if he had a girl friend." They all laughed.

"I think you have the best husband in New York," Sue said wistfully.

"Me, too," Erica smiled.

"What should I do?" Jeannette said. "I think I'll just let things go along."

"The worst that can happen is that it'll end," Sue said.

"Or that his parents find out." Jeannette grinned as she said it.

"You're marvelous, Jeannette." Erica raised her glass. "To you." They all clinked glasses and sat back basking in a warm, merry communion that resided somewhere between companionship and real friendship, a line that moved like the tide, day by day between them, shifting its definition and its allegiances. In an emergency they would all be steadfast. It was the lesser and, in a curious way, more demanding aspect of life that tested them further: the daily round.

Erica hailed a taxi outside P.J.'s totally preoccupied with Jeannette's announcement. That makes him only four years older than Patti. Than Phil. It all struck her as wildly bizarre. It shouldn't. Why should it? Well, maybe it was bizarre.

She got out of the cab, and when she turned around to pay the driver, she noticed how young he was.

"How old are you?" she said.

"I'm twenty-two," he said, "I get off at four, but I could quit anytime."

"It's nothing like that. A friend of mine is thirty-four and she's going with a fellow who's nineteen."

"So?"

"Would you go out with a woman who's fourteen years older than you?"

"Sure."

"I mean seriously . . . have a relationship. . . ."

"If it was the right lady, I would."

"Thanks. Good night."

The cabdriver looked at her questioningly. She realized he still thought it was a pass, and was embarrassed. Male ego, you aren't kidding.

Martin was watching television when she got in. "That was a long meeting," he said.

"They're not meetings. Guess what. Jeannette is going out with a nineteen-year-old boy."

"She's flipped, then."

"Men go out with younger women all the time."

"That's four years older than Patti," he said.

"Where is Patti?" Erica took off her coat and walked over and shut the TV off.

"At the movies, with Phil."

"At the movies, with Phil, necking, you mean," Erica said.

"What?"

"Oh, nothing. I figure they're necking, that's all."

"Patti seems very interested in that creepy kid," Martin said.

"Maybe she is, but she's only fifteen."

"So is he. Hey, maybe you could introduce him to Jeannette."

"Don't be hostile."

"How was the crowd?"

"All three are fine. Except Elaine."

"What's wrong with Elaine?"

"I think she's getting hostile to men."

"I think she always was hostile to men."

"Martin, she adores you. She also has the hots for you."

"She does?"

"Yes, she's waiting for you to leave me so she can get you."

Martin walked over to her and put his arms around her. "I feel sexy," he said.

"Patti's coming home, and I have to get up early tomorrow," Erica said, going upstairs. Martin followed and grabbed her and kissed her, but she broke away. "Elaine said if you were having an affair with another woman I wouldn't know it. I said I would."

"I'm hot," Martin said, grabbing her.

"Well I'm not!" Erica was angry, she didn't know why. "I'm sorry."

"You give me a headache," Martin said.

"Take an aspirin. Unless there's something else wrong with you. How did the checkup go?"

"I have high blood pressure."

"How high?"

"High enough."

"So what do you do?"

"You take pills."

"Oh." Erica heard the doorbell. "That's Patti."

Patti had let herself in by the time Erica was downstairs in her robe. Martin followed her and walked behind her to the refrigerator. "Want a drink?" he asked Erica.

"No, thanks."

"Patti," he said, "how old is Phil?"

"You know how old. Eighteen."

Erica gasped despite herself. "I thought he was fifteen."

"Mother, you are too much."

"Your mother's pal Jeannette is having an affair with a nineteen-year-old kid."

"Good for her," Patti said, nonplussed.

"Would Phil go out with Jeannette?" Martin persisted in a malicious tease.

"You'd have to ask Phil." Patti smiled.

"Don't tell anyone about Jeannette," Erica said to

her daughter, kissing her goodnight, "I'm going to bed."

She went upstairs, heard Martin padding about, turning off the lights, turned on the bed lamp, and began to read. Martin came in, sulking.

"You're behaving like a five-year-old," she said. "I can't turn sex on and off like that. I have feelings, too. It's no good if you make me feel like it's an obligation."

Martin, still gloomy, said, "You're right." Erica read for a few minutes, aware of a weird, unusual tension. "Did the doctor say anything else?"

"Like what?"

"Like anything."

"I told him I'm anxious. He says it happens to men my age. I fantasize all the time."

"About women?"

"About everything. About Tahiti and making mats."

"Is it us, Martin?" she asked, calm, assured it wasn't.

"I don't know. I'm tired of my job, I think. I'm tired of being the boss in my marriage, in my job, everywhere."

"You're not the boss here. You're a boss."

"Maybe that's the trouble."

"Is there trouble?"

"I'm tired. I'm anxious."

Erica put the book down. Usually this kind of conversation came when Martin was in for big money, big money on the market he didn't know he could get back. Lou Silver was usually responsible for that. For persuading Martin to make investments that were risky. Sometimes they worked.

"Are you in a deal with Lou?"

"Several."

"Oh. Martin, are you sure it's not me?"

"I love you." He grabbed her then.

"I'm beginning to feel very lucky to have a man to

come home to. I always feel that way after those meetings." She smiled. "Is it just luck?"

"Luck, and a fabulous body," he said, moving toward her with a new urgency, a recent urgency she recognized in his lovemaking, something with a fine edge of desperation to it. No, she was crazy. She had woken up one night screaming, having dreamt Martin was dying. But she yielded to him now, soft and tender, and then, yielding to something else, a new violence in him, a passion that excited her, called her up higher and higher, led her high, and led her off, falling, falling, soft again.

She turned and shut the light off and kissed him softly. "Good night."

At breakfast the next morning, Patti was unusually quiet. Martin had left early for a meeting. Erica said, "What's up? You're usually noisier."

"Daddy doesn't like Phil, does he?"

"He doesn't dislike him."

"Is he jealous?"

"What do you think?"

"I think he's jealous. Do you think he's worried about getting old?"

"What are you doing, taking a psych course?" Erica was forever amazed by this daughter.

"Well, he keeps joking all the time. He never takes anything seriously."

"You mean he doesn't take Phil seriously, and that bothers you."

"No, it doesn't. I don't take Phil all that seriously, either." She grinned.

"I think you do," Erica said, hugging her.

"Well, I'm not going to marry him, for sure." Patti was getting into her coat.

"Who for sure? Why for sure? Put the lock on the door." Erica gathered up her purse.

"I'm not going to marry anybody," Patti said.

"Why not?"

"Because nobody married is happy."

"Maybe nobody is happy."

"Well, name three happily married couples."

"I don't know three married. But I can't name three happy divorced ones, either." When they were outside the house, Erica kissed Patti on the cheek. "I have to get this cab. I'm late."

Patti kissed her and ran to the corner. She was beautiful, Erica sighed, and she was only fifteen, and she got in the cab. Was Patti disillusioned with marriage? With her parents' marriage? But how could that be? They were a model. Erica didn't want to seem self-satisfied to the point of saturation, but they were, after all.

2

DURING THE CAB RIDE to the gallery, Erica impulsively said to the driver, "Tell me something, Mr. Geller, would you. . . ."

"Call me Sam."

"Sam, would you be upset if you had a thirty-four-year-old daughter and she was going with a nineteen-year-old boy?"

Sam Geller spun effortlessly around the traffic, puffed thoughtfully on his cigar, and said very seriously, "The way I see it, it would be better than if she were going with a nineteen-year-old girl. That's what they do now, you know."

"Did you ever date an older woman, Mr. Geller—er, Sam? Were you ever, uh, interested?" Erica leaned forward. She must be out of her mind, she thought. Why on earth was she trying to have a serious conversation with this man?

"Sure, I dated older women. I'm married to an older woman. My wife is sixty-two."

"How old are you?" Erica said, reaching into her purse for change.

"I'm only sixty," he said, chomping and as serious as when they started. Erica smiled, gave him a tip, and got out of the cab. She meant to get out and then pay—there was something in that style she adored. Elaine had said, "You're going macho on us. I know that's going to be the next hot thing, female machismo."

"How can there be any such thing as female machismo?" Erica had scoffed.

"A certain kind of style—high-heeled boots, paying through taxi windows . . . Think about it." Elaine said.

Erica had decided Elaine was crazy until she met Veronique. Normally any artist having only one name, and that name being Veronique, would have been enough to put Erica off permanently. But when this strange woman, seemingly female but smoking a cigar, with tight dungarees and a special kind of high-heeled boot, covered with rings and leather bracelets, had begun to talk, Erica knew what Elaine meant. But with Veronique, the part that went macho went butch, she lost that female rolling earthiness she had, but she was fascinating. She talked and gesticulated wildly, puffing on this very long, thin dark cigar, her hands moving like magic, her rings catching the light, and those intense eyes burning with every word, every movement. She seemed more like an actress than a painter. At first Herb had said he wouldn't see her. Then he had said he would see her. When he saw her he said he wouldn't take any of her work. By the time she had left, he had agreed to a special opening. It was unique. It was not a sideshow affair. Veronique herself was a total mystery. Herb had completely rewritten her bio for the catalog. Veronique had written, "part Navajo Indian, part rain dancer, part Gypsy, part Polish, part merchant, part Jewess, part charlatan, the bastard daughter of Houdini, conceived in a locked box, sister to the seven winds, daughter of the seven seas, mother to earth and She who is Him, Goddess of the middle continent."

"She's out of her fucking mind," Herb had said and crossed it out.

"I like it," Erica had defended her.

"What's to like? It's not poetry, it's just confusion. It reads sophomoric to me."

"What's so bad with sophomoric?" Erica had said.

"I'm writing born in Paris, educated at the Sorbonne, and self-taught in the American desert."

"Is Veronique French?"

"She speaks good enough French to be French," Herb had said.

When Erica got out of the cab, she saw that Herb had decided most of Veronique's work should be displayed on the gallery floor. "Work" was the best way of putting it. In the middle of the floor was a chair, a hubcap, a motorcycle, rebent, with a Hopi mask on the handlebars, and then through it, around it, playing off the gallery walls and ceilings, were videotaped montages and impressions of the desert. Erica made her way through the crowd building up in the gallery to the rear offices. When she entered Herb's office, she saw Charlie sitting there.

"Hi, Charlie." Erica wondered why he always seemed so glad to see her.

"Hi." Charlie waved a hero sandwich toward her. "Want a bite?"

"No, thanks."

"You see that shit out there? The only reason she's got a show is she's a broad. I can't wait till this movement passes. Jesus Christ."

"You really are a male chauvinist pig," Erica said, looking at him in amazement. "I like it. I think she's original."

"Original is easy," Charlie said. "Good is hard." He took a bite from his sandwich. "But then you know all about that. You are so good. That's your trouble, of course, too good."

"I'm even better than you think," Erica said. "Where's Herb?"

"I know you're good in bed, you won't give me a chance to find out. Don't you ever wanna try something different? Like eating a papaya instead of a peach the rest of your life? Just once, trying a papaya?"

"I'm allergic to papayas. Don't you ever talk about anything else?"

"Hey, Erica, who are we kidding, huh?" Charlie had grabbed her arm. The total feel of him—the Mexican sweater, the boots, the jeans—and the alarming pungency of his hero sandwich repelled Erica. "I mean, there's a little work, there's eating, and there's sex. After that, there isn't anything."

"It's such a pleasure to meet such a romantic mind," Erica said. The phone rang and she picked it up. It was Martin.

"Hi, darling . . . I'd love to. Good. Fifteen minutes. I'll meet you there."

"Who's darling?" Charlie said.

"My husband. He's taking me to lunch." Even as she said it, she felt proud about it. Martin didn't call her for lunch very often, but she always found it wildly flattering, even after all this time. Once he had called her, taken her to lunch, and then checked them into the Plaza. They'd made love all afternoon. She remembered it vividly. She smiled remembering Martin's remark, "Some of your best moments have been in hotels. I can tell. You would have had an interesting life as a chambermaid."

She smiled now.

"He still makes you smile? He still turns you on?"

Erica nodded. "After seventeen years, Charlie."

"He must have a big one," Charlie said, taking a swig of beer, and Erica wanted to sock him.

"You're not a male chauvinist pig after all, Charlie, you're a pig, period." She slammed the door.

As Erica went back out through the front of the

gallery, she thought Veronique ought to be very pleased with Herb. He had really brought in a good crowd. She still had time before meeting Martin, but clearly there was no point in staying there. She would just have a fight with Charlie. Why she bothered, she couldn't imagine. It seemed impossible to ignore him. Erica left the gallery and took a walk down Spring Street, then cut back to Orchard and decided to look into one of the wholesale leather shops. Patti had a birthday coming up, and she wanted to find something special. Sweet sixteen—that was, of course, if sixteen was sweet anymore. Sixteen today seemed like twenty-one when Erica was growing up. She had been thought precocious when she married Martin at nineteen. It had been a bit early. She had been lucky.

She found the store and made her way to the back, where most of the shoulderbags were.

"Can I show you something?" A small dark woman appeared out of nowhere.

"Yes, I'm looking for something for my daughter. She's very young, sixteen; some of these styles seem wrong."

"We have," the woman said assuredly, and turned to a large drawer under the counter.

She brought out a very simply designed caramel-colored leather bag. The leather was beautiful. "It's lovely," Erica said. "How much is it?"

"Ninety, uptown you would pay much more, a hundred and fifty."

"That's a lot for a bag for a kid."

"You're right. So buy it for yourself."

Erica smiled. "Don't think I wouldn't like to."

"So do it. You're only young once."

"I don't think of myself as young."

"Why not? What's wrong with you?"

"Well, I don't think of myself as old, either, but not as young, exactly."

"Well, that's not good thinking. You should think young. You want the bag?" Erica smiled and nodded. She would buy it for herself. It *was* smashing. She was entitled. Actually, Martin had always encouraged her to be more extravagant than she was. The pleasure of being a New York Girl, Elaine had said, "is being rich enough to spend money when you want it, and in New York that means being rich."

"I'm not rich," Erica had protested. "I mean, Martin makes out just fine, but we're not loaded."

"In New York, half a million dollars a year is middle class. Under a hundred thousand is the poverty level. Wherever you are, you're not the poverty level."

It was true. Martin's mother had nearly fainted when she heard what they had paid for their house.

"One hundred seventy-five thousand dollars, and it's not even a new house. For an old house that needs work? I don't believe it. I can't believe it. I always thought my son was very smart, he married a smart girl. Together they did a very stupid thing."

Martin's mother had stood on the sidewalk outside the house, feet astride, and stared at it. "It doesn't look as old as I thought, but for a hundred and seventy-five thousand dollars you ought to at least get a lawn." That was her complete pronouncement, other than to comment that anybody who wanted four floors of stairs in a house must be crazy. Actually, Erica had been surprised when Martin told her they had bought the house. She had liked it, but the purchase of a house had signified something that frightened her. It seemed to her the kind of thing people did when they were "starting a new life" or into their second marriage.

"Or trying to save their first," as Elaine had put it. "Three years before I broke up with Steve, we bought that house in Brooklyn. First we did the woodwork, then we laid in the floor, then we redid the basement.

When we ran out of things to do in the house, we got divorced."

"It was you who walked out, Elaine," Erica had reminded her.

"But to tell you the truth, the last three years I was more committed to the woodwork than I was to him." Smart-ass Elaine. Erica wondered if Elaine knew the truth herself sometimes about what she was saying. When Martin and Erica bought the house on East Seventy-ninth Street, the first thing Elaine said was "Is your marriage O.K.?" Is your marriage O.K.? The New York Question. What was a marriage? It was two people. Were they O.K.? No, that was never the question. It was the ideal people were anxious about, was that O.K., the ideal.

Erica hurried to the Ballroom Restaurant, seeing she was going to be about ten minutes late. She was glad she was meeting Martin because she wanted to get the issue of the summer house settled. Sue had called her the other night to say that she and Roger had taken a house and needed another couple. Erica didn't know how Martin would like sharing, but the idea rather appealed to her. She had visions of long, languorous days on the Cape, walking the dunes, painting, a lot of solo work. Last summer on the Vineyard, Martin had complained that she spent too much time by herself.

"Well, it's not very exciting to sit in the sand while I paint for hours on end."

"No, it's not very exciting," Martin had said. "But I would do it. I think you want to be alone."

"Yes," Erica had said. Martin didn't need that; she could see that Martin essentially never needed to be alone. His work was a flurry of activity, and she had always expected at night he would want some quiet. But he was always ready for a dinner party, hers or someone else's, or what she called marathon phone conversations with his cronies. Marathon, in Erica's view, was any telephone conversation that extended beyond fifteen minutes. She hated the phone for anything other than brief chitchat, and even then.

Martin waved to her as she entered the restaurant. "You're late," he said.

"I know," she said, kissing him. "I went to buy Patti a present and bought one for myself instead."

He smiled. "I'm glad. Let's see it."

Erica undid the bag and pulled out the purse.

"It's good-looking," Martin said. "How much?"

"Ninety," Erica said. "Which is why Patti didn't get it. That's too much for a kid to use as a pencil case."

"I like it," Martin said. "What would you like?"

"I would like that terrific spinach salad," Erica said, "and then a positively outrageous dessert." She reached over and grabbed his hand. "And then, perhaps, the Plaza?" she said. Martin turned visibly pale.

"What made you think of that?"

"You look sick, suddenly. You're smiling, but you look sick."

"Thanks. Any other compliments?"

"Is Lou really tying you up?"

"He really is, Erica." Martin's face looked very grave. He reached over and held her hand. "Do you know I love you very much?"

"I know," she said, feeling suddenly very peculiar. The way he said that.

The waiter brought their salads, and Erica ate hers lustily, feeling very chatty, telling Martin about Veronique's show and Charlie and just generally catching up about the morning. She was so caught up in her own spontaneity she failed to notice he hadn't really touched his salad until the waiter came to clear it away.

"What's the matter? Are you really not hungry?"

Martin grabbed her hand. "I didn't want to insult the waiter. Mine had sand in it."

"Oh, God. Well, there won't be sand in the chocolate cake. It's fabulous, you want some?"

"No, I know a great place for cheesecake. I want to take a walk."

Martin paid the waiter, and Erica slipped into her jacket, and they went out the door. As they were on their way out, Charlie was on his way in.

"Hi, Erica," he said. Erica nodded and tried to push past him, but he planted himself right in front of her. "And you must be 'darling,' " Charlie said.

"Martin, this is Charlie. He leads an imbalanced life. His work has so much finesse he has none left over for himself, which is why we're not staying to talk to him." Charlie stood there while Erica pulled Martin out the door.

"I've never heard you be so bitchy," Martin said when they were on the street.

"He does it to me. He makes me so angry I could tear him up."

"He looks harmless enough."

"He's really a pig," Erica said.

"You don't use words like that."

"It's the only one that fits." She grabbed Martin's hand. "Lead me to the cheesecake shop." They had walked several blocks when Erica said, "Hey, Martin, where are you taking me?"

He turned to her then. His face had a strange look.

"Martin, what is it? Are you ill? You look positively ill. Martin?"

He almost collapsed against her. "Erica, Erica." His face was in his hands. He was shaking.

"Martin!" It was a gasp. Was he going to die? She held him in her arms. "I'd better get a cab," she said.

He pulled her back and held her by the elbows, staring into her face, pale and shaking. "Erica, I'm leaving you! I'm in love with another woman. I've been in love with her for a year. I can't stop. I can't stop!" He was screaming at her, her, her body suddenly rigid, turning to stone, some monolith in the urban landscape, sheer stone as his words fell clanging against her, shattering noises clanking up and down the street, metal on metal, hammering into her. "I'm in love with her," he was gasping practically. "I love you, Erica, but I'm in love with her. I can't take it anymore. I'm sorry. I'm sorry, I didn't mean to do it." Erica stood there, her face cracking into a million pieces. She couldn't talk. Something kept starting up from the middle of her, some energy for sound, but she couldn't make any sounds come out of her mouth until she heard, like a voice from a radio, whispering, "How can you say this to me? How can you say this? Are you crazy? Are you all right? You said you loved me. You took me to lunch." Lunch. Later she would remember that she had said, 'You took me to lunch.' As if lunch were something. She hadn't said, 'After seventeen years of marriage,' she had said, 'You took me to lunch.' But then she just stood there until she could say, "Who is she?"

"You don't know her." In that moment, in that brief transition, Martin looked different. Erica wondered if her eyes had been closed because he looked so different. He looked thinner. His mouth looked odd. She thought he was very ugly. She thought he was so ugly she wanted to throw up. She suddenly felt an overwhelming revulsion, a contempt for him. "Who is she?" Her voice was stone.

"Her name is Marcia, Marcia Brenner. She's a schoolteacher."

"How old is she?"

"Twenty-six. She's very important to me, Erica. I didn't mean to, it just happened."

"Where did it just happen?"

"In Bloomingdale's. I met her in Bloomingdale's.

She was buying a shirt for her father, for his birthday, and I was standing next to her and she needed my advice about the size."

"And you fell in love with her." Erica felt weird, some strange thing was overtaking her.

He nodded. "I've been lying to you for a year. It makes me sick."

"IT MAKES YOU SICK. IT MAKES ME PUKE! PUKE! YOU DISGUST ME. YOU ARE A PIG, A PIG!"

Erica was astounded at the clamor coming from her now. Some strange beast inhabiting her screaming at him.

"Don't scream at me."

"I will scream SCREAM SCREAM SCREAM. YOU MADE LOVE TO ME LAST NIGHT. YOU DID, YOU DID. YOU DID. HOW COULD YOU!" She slapped him furiously, then burst into tears. "A year—oh, God, a year. Lying through a year. Martin, how could you lie like that?" She sat on the steps of a brownstone, crying, trying to keep from retching. "I want to see you for lunch. I love you. Remember the Plaza. Oh, how ironic. How bitterly ironic." Erica began to laugh wildly. Then she screamed, "REMEMBER THE PLAZA!"

"Erica, for chrissake, are you losing your marbles or what?" Martin looked around furtively, which made Erica laugh louder. "What was it, Martin? Why did you fall in love with her? In Bloomingdale's!" She laughed louder. "Bloomingdale's!"

"I'm not going to be interrogated. Look, I said I'm sorry. I am sorry."

"Oh, sure," Erica said, getting her breath. "That's all you have to say. I suppose your bags are packed?"

"I took my clothes out this morning, most of them."

"You do have a daughter." Erica couldn't get the

muscles in her face to work. She heard the words coming now again, but she couldn't feel her mouth move. It must be moving. "Or are you going to leave her a note? 'Met new girl. Will call. Love, Daddy.' "

"ERICA, FOR CHRISSAKE. Do you think this is easy? Do you think it's been easy?" He was furious with her now.

"You want my sympathy, you lousy stinking lying bastard?" She hissed at him, circling around him, her hands moving, fists clenching. Martin backed away from her. "You'd better go, Martin, because I want to kill you very badly. I want to kill you with this." Her hand shot down on the stoop for a brick and, picking it up, she hurled it, missing Martin by an inch.

"For God's sake, Erica." Martin was horrified. "You could have killed me! I see you can't handle this. I'll call you later."

"BASTARD!" Erica screamed, "BASTARD!" as Martin retreated down the block. Then she retched. She held her head and leaned over the curb, retching uncontrollably. Then she sat down on the stoop.

A young kid walked past her. "Lady, are you stoned?"

"No, I'm getting a divorce and I need a cab."

He nodded, went to the corner, and hailed one for her and brought it around.

"You're nice. You're very nice. I appreciate it. What's your name?"

He smiled and handed her her pocketbook. "Salvatore," he said.

"Never mind. You're Italian. They don't know about divorce."

"I know. My mother's divorced," he said quietly. "It's not so bad." He smiled. "You work at the gallery, don't you?"

"How'd you know?"

"I want to be an artist."

She almost smiled. Life was too funny. "Call me in the morning, or come by. I'll see you." She closed the door. "East Seventy-ninth Street, please. Go very slowly down Fifty-ninth Street, driver," she said. "I want to spit on the Plaza."

3

WHEN ERICA got to the house, the shock of what Martin had said had sufficiently subsided for the rage she felt to break through. She walked into the house and systematically broke all twelve of the Doulton china set, piece by piece, their fine blue-and-white edges shattering against the wall, the cat staring in fright from the stairway, the sound of breaking china strangely satisfying.

"There," she said when she was done. "I always hated that damn set, anyway, and Martin made me buy it that week we were in Copenhagen," she said to the cat. "I'm sorry I disturbed you." Thinking, mistakenly, that the shattering dishes had calmed her, she decided to take a shower. Later she would remember that in moments of crisis she always decided to take a shower. The hot, steaming water felt good. She was not, during this time, thinking. She was not thinking, What am I going to do? What went wrong? Did he mean it? She was nowhere. She was just in the shower with the steam rising. When she got out and looked for a towel, another crisis consumed her. Suddenly, panic and fear engulfed her. She couldn't remember where the towels were. Upstairs? Downstairs? In the next room? Where were the towels? She stood there perhaps five minutes trying to determine and then remembered they were stored in the chests under the sink. When she got a towel, Erica, now shivering, stood there with it, thinking, I'm crazy. I'm cracking up. I've gone nuts. I can't take the strain. She could not imagine whether she started drying her feet first, or if she started with her neck, or, no, did you begin with your arms? What way did you approach this drying of the body? What took priority? Were the wet feet dry on the bottom from standing on the rug? Did that mean they were less important? Or was it the chest, the heart, the lungs—should they be dried first? She stood there holding the towel, shivering, shaking, not knowing what to do, feeling temporarily not so much out of her mind as mindless. She had no mind. She had only this shaking body, wet and uncertain of how to proceed in its most fundamental operations. Erica put the towel carefully, very carefully, down on the top of the toilet seat, and still shaking, sat on it. I'll shake dry, she thought, this can't be happening to me. I'm in better shape than this, I don't crack easily. I'm a strong woman. I don't understand what this is. After several minutes, she got up, wrapped the towel around her, and lay down on the bed. She was tired, but she couldn't sleep. She had to get out of the house. She couldn't face Patti yet. Poor Patti. Martin was picking her up after school. God. She wouldn't believe it. Why? What had gone wrong? Erica, thinking of that, felt the cold rage envelop her again. The bastard. All that loving. All that sex, and the whole time he's in love with some nit he runs into at Bloomingdale's. Love. A lot in love. It couldn't be the sex. Could it? Wasn't she active? Didn't she do the right things? Oh, God.

"Hi, Elaine."

"Erica, you sound funny."

"Well, I'm very funny, all right. Are you sitting down?"

"No."

"I'm getting a divorce."

"You're kidding, Erica, what?" Elaine was genuinely bewildered. "You're not kidding. Erica?"

"I'm here. And I'm not kidding."

"I can't believe it. I really can't believe this one. All this time you've been having a hot affair and not telling us. Did you get caught? I can't believe it. I always thought you were the devoted type."

"I am the devoted type. Martin isn't."

"Oh, no. Martin? Martin wants a divorce?"

"That's right. You're catching on. Very good, Elaine."

"Somebody else?"

"Now you have it. A schoolteacher. Her name is Marcia. She was buying a shirt in Bloomingdale's and they fell in love."

"Now I know you're not kidding. Are you kidding? Bloomingdale's?" Elaine shrieked out a kind of painful cry.

"Not Macy's, not Gucci's, not Bendel's. Bloomingdale's."

"I can't stand it. Look, what are you going to do?"

"How the hell do I know? I can hardly get used to this."

"Does Patti know?"

"Of course she knows. He told her himself."

"How is she?"

"She hates both of us. A lot."

"Erica, I feel awful. The bastard. I mean, God, I am really in shock. Did he leave, really? I mean, packed up and all?"

"Yes, he was very efficient. Slipped his bags out of here one by one. All his clothes are gone, anyway. Most of his stuff, shaving stuff, etcetera. A lot of his desk. He did leave his desk, however."

"He'll be back for it."

"Elaine, I think you better come over here. I mean,

maybe it would soften things up with Patti and me. It's a mess."

"I'll be over in an hour." Why Erica wanted Elaine here she didn't know. Her hard-edged presence would seem like a relief somehow in what she felt was clearly becoming a soap factory. Patti crying, her crying. Oh, Christ. What a fuck-up. She'd never fucked up. Not really. This was such a surprise. That was the humiliating part. The surprise. I love you I love you. Maybe . . .

"Elaine . . ." Erica started to say something.

"Yeah."

"Well, thanks."

"What do you mean thanks? How dare you thank me! You know I'd come through for you in a scene like this."

Erica smiled. "I know. It's like the army. When the going gets rough."

"Hey, Erica," Elaine went on. "When did you find out?"

"Yesterday."

"How? I mean, how did he tell you?"

"He took me to lunch."

"He took you to lunch? Oh, my God. Like when you get fired?"

Erica burst out laughing. "I didn't think of that. Oh, Christ, yes, I got fired." Then, still laughing, she burst into tears. "Come over, Elaine, good-bye."

Then she called Herb. She had called up yesterday to tell him she felt sick and she'd let him know today. She would have loved actually going to the gallery. She would have loved to have had something to do, something physical to challenge her, some task that required completion, some visible evidence of progress. She called Herb, unable to tell him the real reason, said she had a bad cold and would be in tomorrow, and then decided to attack her closets.

She set up the iron, took out her underwear, and

began the insane practice of ironing her underclothes. There could not be enough precision in this for her. Neatly, and with almost a demonic conviction, she pressed creases and seams into her panties, smoothed out her bra straps, ironed the two chemises she had, and then in total madness took out her pantyhose and, on a very cool iron, ironed them so they looked as if they came out of a box.

"What are you doing?" Elaine said when she arrived.

"I'm ironing my pantyhose."

"Oh. Well, I guess that's as good as anything. I told Sue. I didn't think you'd mind. She's coming by."

"No, of course I don't mind. Did she faint?"

"More or less. But she's conservative, you know. I said the first thing I was going to tell you to do was to get a lawyer. She says the first thing you should do is relax and not do anything rash. She thinks he'll be back."

"Oh, God."

"You don't want him back?"

"At the moment I don't. What do you think?"

"How'd you react when he told you?"

"I picked up a brick and tried to kill him."

Elaine swatted her on the back. "Good girl, fabulous, Erica. I would not have believed it!"

"Then I called him a pig."

"Oh, wow."

"Then I took a taxi and spit on the Plaza."

"It wasn't the Plaza's fault. I mean, they do a lot wrong, but they didn't make Martin walk out. Or was that where they were doing it?"

"No, that's where Martin and I were doing it."

"What are you talking about?"

"Oh, you know, one day he called me up about lunch and we had lunch and then we rented a room for the afternoon. It was very sexy. Very nice. Big joke."

"When was that? Do you want coffee?"

"No, but make it, anyway. What else is there to do but iron my pantyhose and make coffee? Oh, Elaine, I feel like such a fool."

"Stick to the facts. When was that trip you made to the Plaza?"

"Last March."

"When did he meet this cookie?"

"I don't know. Sometime last year."

"Before March?"

"I think so . . . in January, I think he said. What difference does it make?"

"Well, I don't know what difference it makes. I think Martin is really sadistic. After he meets this other one, he takes you to the Plaza. His wife. It's like having an affair on the affair."

"Oh, I suppose it isn't. What I don't get, what I really don't get, you know, is he's been really turned on all year. I swear."

"Maybe it was an act."

"It wasn't," Erica shouted at her. "Look, Elaine, unless I'm crazy it wasn't an act. He was really coming on. Really coming on."

"Frequency of intercourse can also mean anxiety attack."

"You're really cheering me up a lot."

"Sorry. I'm not good at that. I'm good at the practical aspect. I'll get you a good lawyer." The bell rang. "That must be Sue." Erica pressed the intercom. It was Sue.

"God," Erica said, "she sounds more upset than I am. I'm having a strange case of the calms."

"The pantyhose doesn't sound so calm to me," Elaine said. "It's one step away from paper doilies, you know. You better not spend too much time alone. We'd better take you to the movies tonight."

"What about Patti?"

"We'll take Patti, too."

"She won't go. She'll be out with Phil."

"She'll probably ball him to get even with her father."

"Elaine, for chrissake!"

At that moment Sue knocked, and Erica opened the door. She was overwhelmed at Sue's response—she hugged her and said, "Oh, Erica, I feel awful for you. It's just awful. but we'll help you, I promise we'll help you." She began to cry, and Erica could see that she had been crying already. It was strangely soothing.

Erica began to calm Sue down. "Look, it's all right. I mean, it's not all right. But I'm all right."

"Hi, Sue," Elaine said. "God, you're no help at all. Erica isn't all right at all. When I got here, I found her ironing her pantyhose. You're all falling apart. It always happens. Everybody falls apart when somebody leaves. It's funereal in here, positively funereal. It isn't the end of the world, you know. It's probably good. I know that sounds like the psychology expert, but stop looking at this as if Martin died, Erica." Elaine's voice was sharp. "He nearly died, of course."

"What do you mean?" Sue looked bewildered.

"Erica tried to kill him with a brick."

Sue burst out laughing, tears and all. "You're kidding. Erica!"

"It was just a mad moment," Erica said, shrugging. "I'm sorry I missed."

"Now you're talking," Elaine said.

"Elaine, you're like an army commando. Erica must love Martin very much. And he loves her, I'm sure. I'm sure he'll be back."

"Don't talk reconciliation. It's bad for the nerves. Think 'kick out,' 'nevermore,' 'the end,' and get a good lawyer."

"Elaine, I thought you left Steven. You sound like an old hand at this."

"I am an old hand. I left Steven, but husband *número uno*, the one and only author of the Charlie

Parker blues, Mr. Richard Parker III, left me. And for the worst reason of all."

"What?"

"His secretary. His stupid-assed secretary."

"Did he marry her?" Sue asked.

"Of course not. What happened is what always happens. They, of course, were more devious than Martin. Their affair went on for three years. Three weeks after he left me, they broke up."

"How come?"

"It wasn't interesting anymore. What do you mean how come? I still know that stupid-ass silly tit. Her name is Lesley Hower. She still does her married-man routine. Only this time she's getting herself killed. She's thirty now, see, and it's a little different, and she's been doing this for five years. And I know who it is. And the funny thing is, the wife knows all about it, and that marriage is never going to break up because it's not a marriage. It's an arrangement. Lesley will wake up in about five years."

"Why five years?"

"She'll be thirty-five. Any woman who doesn't make a decision at thirty makes it at thirty-five," Elaine said.

"I don't understand those arrangements at all," Erica said.

"You would if you had one," Sue said. "I need cream for my coffee, Elaine."

"What do you mean?" Erica stared at Sue.

"You have it. I have one. I mean, we sleep together now and then. But he's had affairs for years. I know it. He knows I know it. But he never tells me, and I never ask. They blow over in three or four months and then he's with me, and then another one starts up."

"How do you know when they start?" Erica said. "See, I always thought I would know. I mean, I can't believe I didn't have an inkling of anything. Anything."

"Oh, I always know," Sue said. "Come on, Erica,

you must have known. Maybe you don't want to admit it."

"Maybe she didn't know," Elaine said. "Hell, if I were Erica, I wouldn't know. Everything seemed so goddamned perfect. And then Martin is a bit sadistic."

"What do you mean?" Sue said.

"Well, apparently," Elaine said, "he pulls the old stallion routine when he gets involved."

"Not 'gets,'" Erica said. "This was the only time, Elaine."

"How do you know?"

"I know that." As she said it, she realized she didn't, of course. She also realized she didn't want her friends knowing that she did know, of course. Somewhere. There is no such thing as a perfect life. And she had known. But not this. What, then? What had she known? Something. Something was out of order. She had known it, and she hadn't called it. So much for emotional honesty. She was the one who was always accusing Martin he wasn't honest enough, he tried not to hurt her feelings. And yet she? Had she seen something with Martin dissolve? Had she seen it and allowed it, not caught it? But what was she seeing? And how was she to see? That coldness last summer, that something—she had known, all right. But she had known and not known and not dared to know. Who would dare? Who could dare? Maybe if she had confronted him . . . She had in a strange way eluded Martin, she realized, over the past few years. That summer, painting on the Vineyard, she had been totally into herself. She had not been receptive to him. She didn't know why. Was there a why? A finally verifiable why? She had wanted to be alone, to go down deep into herself. To paint. To be. She had not allowed much for Patti, either, she remembered. She thought, then, of one chilling moment out on the docks, it was a warm evening, and typical of the Vineyard, the fog was beginning to come in, and they had strolled through Edgartown with some friends, and Patti and Phil had been there. She had just met him that summer, and Erica suddenly found him on the edge of the dock with Patti, and out there the fog was getting thicker, and she could barely make out the others down by the restaurant.

"You like Phil, don't you?" Erica had said.

"Yeah."

"Is that all you have to say—yeah?"

"I can't always talk to you when you want to listen. Sometimes I have to talk when I have to talk, you know," Patti had replied almost savagely. "But you're not there for that. You are busy. Painting. You can't be disturbed. Well, now I can't be disturbed. I need my privacy, too."

It had been so harsh, and sudden. Erica had been jolted by it. She had realized then, she had been more removed than she wanted to acknowledge. She should have come alone. Without them. But then, for those parts of the day when she was not occupied with her work, what then? She knew what happened. She became strangely sexual when she was alone, out on the beach, painting. If Martin were not there, she felt she would have gotten involved with someone. It startled her now to think of it, sitting here with her two friends, swearing she hadn't had the faintest notion of it, swearing it to herself, partly, and thinking that that summer on the Vineyard she would have slept with another man, was ready to. Probably. And that maybe Martin felt it. Why wasn't Martin the right one, then? Why, the sex had been good, she insisted, that summer, as it always was. But it was true, things had been better since last year. When she sensed that urgency in Martin—she did sense it—she had mistaken it for a renewed passion when it was really his last, she imagined, desperate attempt to convince himself he wanted Erica. He didn't. That meant he didn't want her and was fucking her night and day to prove to himself he did. Oh, God. She felt sick. She was sick.

Sue and Elaine were looking at her.

"You look like you're going to be sick," Elaine said.

"I am." Erica went to the bathroom and closed the door. She was sick. Oh, Christ. Sick. Sick from what? Lies made you sick. Her mother's friends used to say, when she was a child, never to lie or you'll get sick. The Lord will punish you. The Lord of your own mind. The convictor. You paid heavily for fooling yourself. But how did you know? Erica leaned against the door, tears slipping from her eyes.

"Are you O.K.?" She heard Sue's voice.

"Yes," she said, crying.

And they let her be. It was twenty minutes later when Erica came out of the bathroom, composed. Elaine was in the kitchen making something, and Sue was in the living room reading.

"Are you cooking?" Erica said to Elaine.

"Yes. Chicken. We're staying for dinner. And then we're going to the movies."

"Patti should be home now," Erica said, looking at her watch.

The buzzer rang, and Erica pressed the intercom to find it was the cleaners with Martin's coat.

"Elaine," she hissed, "it's the cleaners. What should I do?"

"The cleaners?"

"Yes, they have Martin's coat. I don't want to tell the cleaner he's left, for God's sake."

Elaine nodded, looking puzzled. Erica realized she was whispering.

"Well," Elaine said, "just tell him you'll pick it up. That's all."

"I, uh, Mr. Benton will be by for it later," Erica said.

"Yes, yes, no, just take it back." TAKE IT BACK, YOU STUPID-ASS DELIVERY BOY, she wanted to yell. Take it back. Oh, God, how stupid. She would have been mortified to tell the delivery boy he didn't live here anymore. Mortified. God. Was it going to be like this forever?

There was a noise at the door. The lock turned and Patti walked in.

"Hi, Sue," she said. "Hi, Elaine. Well, I see the divorce emergency committee has arrived. Guess I'll come back later," and she turned toward the door.

"Stop right where you are," Erica said. "These are my friends, and I will not have you being rude to them."

"Are these two of the happily married you were trying to think of the other day?" Patti asked.

"Cut the crap, Patti," Elaine said. "Your mother's having as hard a time as you are. I know it hurts. Of course it hurts. But it isn't the end of the world. You'll still see your father, you know. He didn't die. I wish everybody would stop acting as if somebody died."

Patti turned back and put her books on the table. "I'm sorry, Elaine. I just don't like coming home very much."

"We're going to a movie," Sue said, "after dinner. Would you like to come?"

"No, thank you. The company looks like a gathering of the losers to me."

"Patti!" Erica had never heard her talk like this.

"Let her go," Elaine said. "Patti, you better learn this, and you better learn it early. Women without men aren't losers. The losers are the women who think being without a man is being a loser. You won't understand that for ten years, but give it a crack in your spare time." She turned then and went into the kitchen.

"Women's lib is a crock," Patti said. "Marriage is a crock and so is just about everything else. I'm going upstairs while you all can console my mother how liberated she's going to feel." Patti stomped upstairs.

"She's really upset," Sue said.

"I find her rather charming," Elaine said. "She certainly lacks any of those phony social veneers that most people acquire in life in order to make it more pleasant."

"She's angry, Elaine," Erica said. "Especially at me. She thinks it's my fault. Actually, so do I."

"Uh-oh, that's the beginning of the end. Look, Erica, it isn't your fault. It's nobody's fault when a marriage falls apart."

"That's too easy, Elaine. It probably was my fault. I obviously wasn't paying attention to something I should have been."

"Baloney," Elaine said. "That's like saying if the sky were green instead of blue it would match the grass. It isn't. It's part of it that you weren't paying attention, if that's what you weren't doing. Maybe you were both lying to save something that was just going. Going."

"But why do things go? They don't just get up and go. Something must happen, Elaine. Something must have happened."

Sue came in. She shrugged. "Natural erosion, I think."

Erica shook her head. "It's something else. It's not natural. You turn off maybe a little somewhere along the line, you stop wanting to know if anything's wrong, because it's so much nicer to think that everything's right. You stop wanting to have to deal. You settle in."

"*You* settle in. Maybe everyone doesn't," Sue said.

"You've settled in," Elaine said to Sue.

"I haven't settled in at all." Sue's voice was full of protest. "I know what's going on. Nothing gets past me."

"Bullshit." Elaine had been drinking, Erica now realized. She hadn't noticed at first, but while the rest of them were having coffee, Elaine had been sipping her martini. Since she arrived, she'd had a few. And when she arrived, she had probably had a few.

"Nothing gets past you," Elaine said. "Plenty gets past you. Well, something important is getting by. You can count on it." Sue looked startled. Erica sensed something about to go wrong.

"Elaine, take it easy. Nobody can catch everything, for God's sake. Some relationships are good, some are lousy, some are great. I thought mine was great. Martin thought it was great. Only obviously it wasn't so great. So nobody knows everything. There is such a thing as fate. Things do just *happen.*"

"Have it your way." Elaine raised her glass.

Patti arrived suddenly in the living room. "Did someone mention dinner?" she asked, looking composed.

"Yes," Erica said. "Elaine makes that great chicken. It should be done. Isn't it, Elaine?"

"Yes." Elaine sauntered into the kitchen. "Everybody sit down."

"How did she get to be such a great cook?" Sue asked, obviously wanted to change the subject.

"Her mother, I think," Erica said. "Also, she never gives you her recipes."

"I give plenty of recipes," Elaine said, bringing in a gloriously shiny, browned chicken.

"You do not," Sue said, her voice sounding falsely animated. "You always change the ingredients. I've never been able to make those cream puffs you make. I know you leave something out."

"A girl can't give away all her secrets," Elaine said, smiling and serving the chicken.

Erica knew she couldn't eat a thing, but she was so

grateful to them for coming over. They acted as if they had all the time in the world, but she knew she had interrupted something. Nobody in the city is ever doing "nothing." She poured some wine. Then she turned to Patti and said, "Would you like some?" She never offered Patti wine, and she knew the minute she said it she shouldn't have.

"No. I do not need consolation as badly as the rest of you. You keep saying you never did anything wrong. But you did." She turned to Erica. "I heard that absurd conversation. Things just happen"—she was hissing ferociously—"WELL, NOTHING JUST HAPPENS. YOU DID IT. YOU DID SOMETHING. YOU MADE HIM GO AWAY," she screamed at Erica, tears springing to her eyes.

"Patti, I . . ." Erica stood up, embarrassed, not sure what to do, so unlike Patti to have an outburst.

"YOU DID IT. YOU MADE HIM GO AWAY. YOU MADE HIM. IT WAS YOUR FAULT. YOU DID SOMETHING WRONG. WRONG, WRONG!" Patti was screaming now, hysterically, tears all over her face. Elaine and Sue seemed frozen. Erica slapped her.

"DON'T TOUCH ME!" Patti slapped her mother hard back across the face, "I HATE YOU!" and ran, bolting out the door.

Erica stood, transfixed by her sudden humiliation, by her concern for Patti, by her sudden sense of nakedness, of exposure, that she was nothing. Nothing. Martin had gone. Her fault. Three women. Nothing. They stood there, each of them seemingly caught in the horror of the moment. It was your fault. Women. The fault of women. Their collective fault that men left them. They felt Patti's cry as a curse. It resounded deep within each of them. Even Elaine, knowing she shouldn't believe it, shuddered at the way the girl had cried out. *You did something wrong*. How often had they said it. How often had they felt it. Wrong. There was something they were doing wrong by the very fact that they existed. They were wrong. The wrong race.

Sue was crying.

"I feel sick," Elaine said. "Erica, are you all right?"

"I'm going to call Phil in a few minutes. She doesn't even have a coat. I'm beginning to hate her. On top of everything else, in the course of two days I am beginning to hate my own daughter."

"You better get a shrink," Elaine said. "This is getting too heavy for us. I can tell."

"I think Patti will go over to Phil's house," Erica said.

None of them said anything. It was impossible to eat. After a few minutes, Elaine got up and put the food in the refrigerator, cleared the table, and started to do the dishes. Erica called Phil and asked him to call her as soon as Patti got there. When a half hour went by and he hadn't called, Erica said, "I guess I have to go out and look for her. I mean, it's cold out."

"Christ, Erica, she's not stupid," Elaine said.

"But she's so angry," Sue said, "she might go out and get pneumonia just to get even with everything."

The phone rang. "Yes," Erica said.

It was Phil. "She's here, Mrs. Benton. I told her I was calling you. She's mad as hell."

"Let me talk to her," Erica said.

There was a pause. Then Phil's voice. "She won't talk to you, Mrs. Benton. I think I better try to talk to her myself."

"Thank you, Phil. Thanks. Look, I'm glad she's there. I think I'm going out. I'll be back around ten o'clock."

"Uh, O.K. Sorry, Mrs. Benton, I'm sorry about Mr. Benton and everything."

"Thanks, Phil. Thank you." She hung up the phone. Funereal was right. Oh, God, what a lot of crap all of a sudden.

"Let's go to the movie," Erica said, suddenly desperate at the three of them in the house, the desperateness of the three of them in the house, feeling naked and alone and as if they were no comfort at all. As if Patti's outburst had confirmed they were nothing. Manless and alone. Oh, God, all the clichés were true. Were true.

Erica got her coat and waited by the stairs. Suddenly she couldn't bear the idea of going to the movies with Elaine and Sue. When they came out, she said, "Look, I love you, you've been great, but I have to be alone again, I have to go for a walk. I'm sorry." A slow shadow passed over Elaine's face. She knew.

"O.K.," Elaine said. "Don't slash your wrists. Get drunk. Get drunk, get laid, or get angry," Elaine said, "but don't let him wipe you out." Her eyes were very bright. She grabbed Erica. "Don't let him destroy you, Erica. You're not as strong as I thought." She held Erica so tightly Erica thought for a moment Elaine was going to kiss her. Then she released her. In that moment in Elaine's face Erica saw the depth of her fear of men, her fear of loving men. "Don't let him destroy you, Erica." Elaine. The first one walked out, Elaine walked out on the second, and continued to walk. Walked out on her friends in a sense, Elaine of the hard, steely edge, Elaine carooming through life like a trucker, hard, talking tough, knowing that if she ever hit something soft at the speed she ran, the intensity of the race, she'd be dead. She had said to Erica, "When Parker left me, I was creamed, I mean really creamed. I never felt like such shit in all my life. I used to get up in the morning and throw up just because I was so disgusted with myself. Well, somebody pulled me out of that, and I promised that somebody that I'd never let that happen to me again. And I won't." And instead of the fear, the depth of vulnerability that had been there, there was now a sharp, steely edge, a raw anger that erupted uncontrollably at the first sign of Elaine's old victim, her self.

Erica walked out on the street alone, watching Elaine and Sue walk toward Third Avenue. She turned and went the other way. She thought about Elaine. She really did love her. Elaine's face, the expression, the depth of feeling had touched Erica. She could not help at the same time wondering if she would ever wind up like Elaine. She couldn't bear it. For all of her breezy, smart talk, Elaine never really encountered life, or, Erica was sure, love. She had an attitude toward life, and that was how she dealt with it.

Erica walked over to Fifth Avenue and then along the park. The trees were covered with snow, and there was the beginning of the moon. It looked beautiful to her. But she felt sad. She felt very, very sad. She felt it in her feet, which couldn't walk as fast as they once did or as lightly; she felt almost as if her shoes were magnetized, holding her to the ground, pinning her. She was worried about Patti. And she felt guilty. God, she felt guilty. And angry. Angry at Martin. When she thought about it, she felt a heat envelop her. She would like to kill him. She really would like to kill him. And then something else. Something she hadn't expected. A kind of contempt settled in, a contempt for his lying to her. She had thought he would not lie to her, that somehow he was above that. Martin. That somehow his manhood was above that. He had lied to her. Why? Because he was afraid? Why should she feel such contempt? Couldn't she see he was in pain that day? His call last night. She had hung up on him. She couldn't bear the sound of his voice. She knew she would have to see him again. They would have to meet, they would have to talk. But this strange ugly image persisted in her mind. Revolting. Martin was, on some level, absolutely revolting to her.

She walked all the way down Fifth to the Doubleday bookstore at Fifty-seventh Street. She went in, browsed aimlessly through the new fiction, bought a new novel that was supposed to explain the sexuality of women in a new way, and hailed a cab home. She was exhausted.

4

THE NEXT MORNING, Erica woke up feeling refreshed. Perhaps there was something to be said for a bad novel, half a bottle of brandy, and final reconciliation with your daughter. Patti had walked in last night, a very sad, subdued little girl. She had crept up to Erica's bedroom and put her arms around her mother.

"I'm sorry. I'm sorry for what I said. I didn't mean it." She had not cried, she had just lain in Erica's arms, wanting comfort, wanting reassurance, wanting what Erica felt then at that moment she could give her.

"He didn't leave you, Patti. He's still your father," she had said. "He left me. He didn't even mean to do it. Things happen to people when they get older. They get scared."

"Scared of what?" had come the muffled question. Patti's head was buried in Erica's shoulder.

"We don't know, baby," Erica had said softly. "They just get scared."

"Daddy isn't the scared type."

She heard sniffles then. And for once in her life Erica had the perfect answer for her budding intellectual daughter, an answer to reassure, an answer to put it all in perspective. "I mean scared like Camus was scared. Taking risks." Patti had relaxed in her arms.

Later, she thought of the irony of it. The irony of making a hero out of Martin, for whom she felt such contempt. She had lied heroically to Patti. And she was glad. Secretly she wanted to kill him. The impulse occurred again and again. But more than kill. She wanted to slice him up.

But that morning, it was as if a storm had cleared. One storm, anyway. Erica felt finally that on some level she could deal with it. Deal at least with the questions that would come, the prying, the embarrassment. As she got dressed, she was aware she was going out of her way to look good. Was that insane, or was that insane? As if people would peer at her and say, "Did he leave you because you were ugly?" That somewhere she knew she thought Martin must have fallen in love because this girl was prettier. Stupid. As stupid as it was to think that somewhere she thought that it was a question of who was the prettiest girl. She hated herself for belittling herself this way. She couldn't imagine what was happening. It was crazy. She looked in the mirror. What looked back looked good. She said to the image, "I always thought you had confidence. But you didn't. Not very much, anyway. Well, you have to get some." She stared into the mirror for a long time and then went downstairs to get Patti breakfast.

Patti was up, breakfast had been made, coffee was poured, and Patti was reading.

"Hi, Mom." Erica could tell Patti did not want to talk about last night.

"Hi. It was nice of you to do breakfast."

"Yeah. Well, I was up early. I got hungry." Patti's head did not lift from the book.

"What are you reading?"

"Freud . . . I think he's crazy."

"Who isn't?" Erica said, sipping her coffee. "Why are you reading such heavy stuff?"

"I had a fight with Phil last night. I'm trying to understand him."

"What about?"

"Daddy. He was defending him. He says he understands. He defended you, too. He kept talking about the forces of life."

"Which are?"

"Who knows? They sound good."

"Did you make up?"

"Yeah. Sort of. I mean, we left on sort of good terms. I'm still mad."

"At Phil or Daddy?"

"I hate Daddy. I'm mad at Phil. But to tell you the truth"—Patti put the book down—"I have the strangest feeling that it wouldn't matter to me at all if they both dropped dead. I don't care about them. I don't want to see him again."

"Who? Phil or your father?"

"Both of them."

"You're being crazy."

"I know." Patti started to laugh and cry at the same time. "Do you want to see him again?"

Erica said, "I have to. I think he'll come here to see you."

"I mean"—Patti chose the words carefully—"would you take him back? I mean, Phil said it might be a middle-aged fling."

"You want him to come back," Erica said, "I know. But it's over, Patti. For good. You'd better get used to it." At that moment the phone rang.

Patti jumped up. "Hello?" She seemed excited. Then, "Oh, hi, Phil. What do you want?"

Erica took her coffee back upstairs. She could hear Patti. "I don't know, Phil, I'm late. Call me tonight." Erica heard Patti hang up the phone and get her coat on. "I'll see you tonight, Mom," she called and was out the door.

Erica knew Patti would be all right, whatever all right was. She wouldn't crumble. She worried about herself, though. She stared at herself in the mirror. "Balls, said the queen. If I had 'em, I'd be king."

She finished her coffee and got ready to go to the gallery. She took the subway, not wanting to think about why, but knowing full well why. Knowing that in the midst of all of this it had suddenly occurred to her that she had no money. None of her own money. Had never had her own money. That when she got home that night she had a twenty-dollar bill in her wallet. That was it. She knew she could draw a check from the checking account, but she was suddenly, sharply aware that it was Martin's money she was taking.

Taking. She felt on the take. Oh, brother. She who had never had a problem about "his" money and "her" money. When her father died he had left her a small amount, ten thousand dollars, and now she wondered what had happened to it. That was years ago. It had gotten used up somehow. Her mother had said to her, "You really should have some money of your own, you know," with embarrassment, hesitantly, "in case, well, you never know. A woman likes to do things sometimes without her husband knowing." Erica had scoffed then. That was back in the old days, Ma, when women weren't liberated, when marriages weren't honest. Honest. Her fists clenched at the thought of it. And me feeling sorry for him, she thought, thinking it was all about Lou. Lou's investment schemes, and Martin saying, "Yes, I'm into Lou for a lot." Bullshit. More lies. She tried to read the paper but the train was too crowded. Soon she gave up and gave in to her thoughts. I guess, she thought, Elaine is right. I really had better get a lawyer. She wondered who she could call. She hated using someone else's lawyer, like Elaine's. It felt like using someone else's bed sheets. She supposed that was stupid, too. Everything was stupid. Erica sighed as the train pulled into her stop. Boy, two days ago I had a perfect life, a perfect ass. I'll probably get fat, my ass'll drop, and I'll spend the rest of my days feeling sorry for myself. But even as she climbed the stairs, she knew she wouldn't. That was how it was going to be, she could tell. Total despair, small rushes of enthusiasm, of feeling hopeful. Hating Martin. God, she hated him. And then the forgetting. When she woke up at first this morning, for a second she forgot he wasn't supposed to be there. She reached over for him and felt a space and was alarmed. Where was he? Then she remembered.

When she walked into the gallery, Herb said to her, "Boy, you look sick. What happened to you?"

"I thought I looked good. Thanks for cheering me up. I'm not sick. I'm getting divorced."

"You're what?"

"Why is it everybody has to ask me to repeat it? Is it so unusual? Doesn't everybody do it?"

"Yeah, but you're not everybody. Come on in here." He beckoned Erica into his office. "So what is this business about getting a divorce?" he said kindly. "So you had a fight. So it happens." He looked so worried, Erica almost burst out laughing.

"Herb, don't try to be nice to me. It's over. That's all. My husband left me for another woman."

"The son of a bitch"—Herb stood up—"I'd like to get my hands on him. . . . Erica, you're a terrific girl. This happens to people . . . maybe he'll get over it."

Erica was touched by his concern and also angered by it. Why did everyone expect her to take him back? As if the real loss was losing Martin, not her? Because he was the one that walked? Was that it? He turned to her now.

"He actually left you? Walked out?"

"That's how they do it," Erica said. "Somebody has to walk out."

"I could never do it," Herb said.

"No," Erica said, "neither could I. But if things go bad, somebody has to. Maybe it takes more nerve to walk than to stay, Herb."

"Look, anything I can do?"

"Yes," Erica said, surprised at herself. "Give me a raise."

"A raise?" Herb looked shocked. "Erica, you think I can?"

"Think it over, Herb. I'm going to have to live on something." She had surprised herself.

"Yeah, well, sure. I mean, he's got to leave you something, right? Have you got a good lawyer?"

"I don't even have a lawyer," Erica said. "I don't know from lawyers, Herb. I mean, the idea is awful, isn't it?"

"Yeah, it's awful. But you better call one. I'll give you the name of a divorce guy."

Erica put her coat away and went out into the back to sort through some canvases. Herb came in in a few minutes and handed her a card. "Here, he's supposed to be good, call him up, Simon Al Leventhal, Attorney-at-Law."

"Well"—Erica brushed off her hands—"here I go."

Mr. Leventhal was not in, but his polished secretary informed Erica that he did not handle divorce suits. However, Mr. Marin did, and she'd be glad to give her Mr. Marin's number. So Erica dialed Mr. Marin. She got through.

She gave her name and was about to explain the circumstances when Mr. Marin said, "Mrs. Benton, how much did your husband earn?"

"What?"

"How much was your husband's annual income?"

"Is that important to know? I mean, I can pay you if that's what you mean. I can pay you for the phone call, anyway, Mr. Marin."

The lawyer's oily voice became apologetic. "No, Mrs. Benton, I know that, but I need to have some idea of the size of the case."

"I don't want any money. I need some for a while, of

course, to live on, but forget it if you think I'm out to get him."

"Look," the lawyer said, "I understand what an emotional time this is for you, but if you give me some idea of your husband's income, I can give you some guidance. Otherwise, I can't."

"About a hundred thousand dollars a year, I think. I really don't know, but I think around that."

"I see"—she heard the lawyer thinking—"and the circumstances?"

"Circumstances?"

"What happened? Did you leave, or did he, or what?"

"He left."

"Were you having an affair?"

This was a bit much, Erica thought.

"No, of course not."

"Was he?"

"Yes. That's why he left."

"Are you sure?"

"Of course I'm sure. That's why he left. Look, I really don't want to go into this on the phone. I . . ."

"Look, Mrs. Benton, I want to represent you. This is a great case. He walked, and he's worth a quarter mil, and you know he's having an affair. I work on a fee basis and a percentage of the award. Be in my office at two o'clock because I'm catching a four o'clock plane to Washington."

"Mr. Marin, go fuck yourself," Erica said and hung up, shaking. Good God, ghoulish she knew it would be, but this was worse than ambulance chasing.

Herb came back into the office. "How'd you make out?"

"I didn't. I'm forgetting about the divorce. What do I need a divorce for?"

"I don't know. You told me. Either you're getting a divorce or you're getting a reconciliation. You've got to be getting something."

"Headache. That's what I'm getting. A headache. Sorry, Herb. Got any aspirin?"

"Yeah, sure. Look, Erica, you sure you know what you're doing?"

"No. Do *you*, Herb?" She smiled.

"O.K., O.K., I'll leave you alone. Look, Erica, anything you need, I'm here. I can't work in a raise right now, but anything else, believe me, you can count on Herb." He patted her shoulder.

"Herb"—Erica looked him straight in the eye—"I don't need love, Herb. I need money." He sighed and turned away. "Think it over," she said. "I have to hang some canvases." Work. Work. Work was what she needed. All that morning Erica stretched and nailed and hung, glorying in the sheer physical quantity of it all. Then she took out a broom and swept out the entire back of the gallery, cleaned the bathrooms, and washed the floor. At four o'clock, she was tired.

"I'm going home, Herb. I'll see you tomorrow."

As Erica was leaving, Charlie was walking in. He grabbed her arm. "Hey, beautiful, hang around. I just got here."

"Let go, Charlie." She was surprised she didn't try to pull away.

"Come on, let me buy you a drink."

"I'm really in a hurry."

"A drink won't take long. Come on." He pulled her into the street, and, surprisingly, she didn't resist him. There was something about him that made her go. She really couldn't stand him, but she was going.

Erica ordered a beer, and Charlie drank vodka.

"I think that's pretentious, drinking vodka," Erica said.

"What's pretentious? That it's Russian?"

She nodded, smiling despite herself.

"I think it's pretentious to think it's pretentious."

"Hey, Charlie," she said, teasing, "why do you always wear this macho stuff?" She reached out and touched his wrist.

"What's macho?" He was wary now.

"You know, all the leather stuff, the jeans, the boots —you wear everything but spurs." She started to laugh. Then she said, "Tell me, Charlie, are you insecure about your masculinity?" She was surprised at the meanness of it herself.

But he matched her. Leaning forward, he said, "I must be. I always go for the ball breakers." He got up then. "I don't need a drink to get my balls broken, Erica. It's my own fault. I think from now on I'll leave you alone." He turned and walked out the door. She caught up with him and walked beside him, saying nothing.

"Erica, get lost." Charlie kept walking.

"I know you like me, Charlie."

"Erica, you're a real prick, you know it?" And then he turned to her, serious. "And you're too pretty to be a prick. You know, you're pretty. You shouldn't act like that." He left her staring after him in the sun.

"I'm pretty. I shouldn't act like that," she said, shaking her head, and then she began to laugh.

5

IN THE NEXT TWO WEEKS, Erica refused to talk to Martin at all. She knew eventually she'd have to see him. Money, for one thing. She hated the idea. She realized for the time being she wanted nothing more than never to see him again. Ever.

She knew, slowly, what was happening. That Martin, whoever her Martin was, that corny phrase, had been an Ideal. A Perfect Martin. She would never have said, "He's perfect," but somewhere in some curious way she felt it. She knew now she felt it because of the startling imperfection he now revealed. He seemed to her now to be nothing more than a creep. A creep. She was staggered that she could have married him. But that was only part of what was happening to her. She was becoming aware that in an awful way she was beginning to hate men. She sometimes thought she had always hated men. All men. Elaine had said to her, "You know, one of these days you'll feel like going out on a date, seeing a man," and Erica had said, "Forget it. I wouldn't care if I never saw another man," and she had meant it. She knew it wouldn't last, but the surprising thing, at least to her, was that it was there at all. It was rather startling to discover the intensity of her feeling. When men got next to her, crowded her in elevators, she wanted to reach out and slug them. Slug them all and push them out of the elevators, off the trains, open the conductor's booth and run the damn train herself.

Men. She really wished they'd fuck themselves off the face of the earth.

That was today. Tomorrow, she didn't know. Yesterday, she forgot. The one thing that kept her solid was Patti. Patti seemed real, in her anger, in her sadness, in her independence. Her youth seemed to give her a sense of proportion that Erica felt eluded her. Patti was sad, Patti was frightened, but Patti was not thirty-four and unsure. Never held a real job. Didn't know how to deal with herself. All the independence that Erica had ever experienced had been in relationship to Martin. She knew somewhere that part of the hatred she felt for him was that he had now revealed to her how weak she was. And dependent. She never would have used those words before. Never.

By the end of the third week, when Erica noticed a persistent and enveloping tiredness, when her stomach was constantly upset, she decided she'd better go to Dr. Jacobs. Maybe he would give her something to relax her. She really wasn't feeling too energetic. It bothered her, because somewhere in her energy had always been her motivation. Now she felt kind of aimless. If it hadn't been for Patti, she thought she might have drifted away. Patti and her own mother. Oh, was that something to deal with. Erica's mother had called from California, and Erica, composed now, had finally told her. She couldn't bring herself to tell her mother why. She thought at the time she was protecting Martin. Her mother had always been crazy about Martin, but she realized later she couldn't bear to tell her mother that she, perfect, beautiful Erica, had been spurned, cast aside for another one. It was not because it would hurt her mother; it was because it would humiliate Erica in front of her mother. It was ridiculous, but Erica felt the shame of her abandonment so deeply in relationship to her mother that she calmly said, "I left, Mother. I had to leave. Martin understands. It happens to people. The marriage wasn't what I wanted. I felt imprisoned. I need my freedom." Her mother had sighed, said she would fly East, begged Erica to come to California, and expressed such total concern that Erica relented and said she'd try to fly out in the next month.

"I'm sending you a ticket. Do you need money?"

"No, I don't need money."

"Did he leave you some money, at least for a while?"

"It's all taken care of, Mom." But it wasn't. That was what Erica was dreading. She was going to have to see him and ask him for money. If he had any finesse, he would have sent her money, but he didn't. She was going to have to beg for it. At least that was what she imagined. At the thought, an overwhelming wave of fatigue assailed her. She called and made an appointment with the doctor.

When Dr. Jacobs had finished his examination, he smiled at Erica and said, "If you won't sue me, Erica, I'd say that off the record you're in beautiful shape. Also in excellent health."

"Thanks. When will we have the result of the blood tests?"

"In a few days. But I doubt there will be anything. Nothing organic."

"Then why am I so tired?"

"It's called divorce."

"Can't you give me a Valium or something?"

"I'd rather see you smoke a joint than take Valium," Arthur said, leaning back and smoking on his pipe.

"Look, Arthur, I've got to do something. I came here because I thought you'd give me some pills. I forgot who you were, Mr. Anti-Pill himself. So at least give me the name of a psychiatrist. I have to do something."

"Do you smoke grass?"

"No, my daughter does. Do you?"

"Once in a while. Did you feel tired before all this

happened? Look, Erica"—Arthur leaned back for one of his fatherly lectures—"there's nothing wrong with feeling lousy when a husband walks out on you. You'd be crazy if you felt good about it. But it's only been a few weeks. Time is the best healer. I'm not saying you shouldn't see a psychiatrist if you want to, but. . . ."

"But you don't think I need one, clearly."

"Are you seeing other men?"

"Don't be ridiculous," Erica almost snapped at him.

"It's not ridiculous. It's called natural in some quarters. You will eventually, you know. There's nothing shocking about it."

"I'm not in the mood for men. In fact, I'm so much not in the mood, I think I should see a psychiatrist."

"I'm not talking about sex. I'm talking about companionship."

"Oh? Are there male companions out there who don't want to get laid?"

Arthur leaned forward and smiled. "You're my last patient. You could have a drink with me."

"Is that a pass, Arthur?"

"No," he said relaxedly, "just an invitation to have a drink."

"Why didn't you ever ask me to have a drink when I was married?"

"You didn't need a drink when you were married."

"It's a pass, Arthur," Erica said, annoyed and standing up, "a definite fucking pass." Erica got up, and slammed the office door.

Elaine said she had to come to P.J.'s especially because she didn't feel like it, a logic Erica both respected and abhorred. She really didn't think she could walk past that single line of men without hitting every goddamned one of them smack across the jaw. Hitting jaw by jaw all those handsome, smiling rows of perfect white teeth. But she went. And she looked good. If she hated men so much, she couldn't figure out why she spent forty-five minutes doing her hair and her makeup. And she also couldn't understand why, having spent forty-five minutes doing her hair and her makeup, when she walked past that line of men and one of them said, "Hello," she said, "Fuck off."

"I'm getting abrasive. Worse than Elaine," Erica said when she got to the table. "I say 'fuck' a lot."

"Well, that's not too bad," Elaine said. "I mean, it has more class than 'up yours.' 'Up yours' is really crude. Stay away from it."

The waiter arrived at that moment to take their order, and Elaine, who had been drinking quite a lot, clearly, before she arrived, couldn't resist and said, "Up yours." The waiter backed off and they all roared. Even Jeannette. Jeannette, gasping through the laughter, said, "Oh, he's not insulted. We're like all those awful men who pour beer down the front of waitresses," and this sent them into peals of laughter. Their talk of men was more savage and funnier than ever. The mood had shifted. Now Erica was one of them, and the ideal woman, the ideal life, the perfect marriage having been put aside, the rawness of their anger revealed itself. Erica was not the only one who hated men. Each of them in their own way, in their own fascination with, dedication to, seduction of, worship or adoration of, and enslavement to—in each of their own ways they worshiped, Erica thought, at the shrine of men. And so they hated their gods. Tonight the mobs were rebelling, the king's throne was toppling. The king, of course, never would know about it, and as she drank more and more beer, Erica realized the king probably had never known about it, but that on some level of silent communication, repressed rage always found its comrades, its routes, that women had always plotted their survival in times of hurt, abandonment, insecurity, widowhood, poverty, that somehow their bonds to their children had bound them to each other. Erica felt deep among them a kind of sharing of predicament she had never known before. She had never thought of herself as part of them, really. She had been Erica. She had been Different from them. Better. She now realized the full force of her Superiority. She had had a man. One man. A permanent man. A man with money who took care of her, adored her, and loved her well. That was the supreme prize, to capture all of those things. And she had had it, and now she didn't have it, and in their laughter, their drunkenness, their hostility, their desperation, they each knew they needed that to survive, if not all of them, then one of them. They were scared together, and with her. Someone, one of them had to have a perfect life. Someone, one of them had to be making it loud and clear. This made the others interesting. But if they were all in the same boat, a kind of desperation engulfed them. They didn't want to be failures. That was what part of this laughter tonight was about. That was what part of Elaine's drunkenness was about.

"Erica, Erica, for chrissake, don't get poor."

"Stop feeling sorry for me," Erica had said.

"For me. I feel sorry for me. I couldn't stand to see you poor. I wouldn't love you anymore. I'd run away from you, Erica. You have to have money. Especially now. Especially now. Without a man. You have to have money."

"Poor Martin," Jeannette had said, and they had jumped on her.

"Don't feel sorry for Martin, for chrissake," Elaine had whipped out at her.

"But I do. Erica will make it," she said placidly.

"Why?" Erica asked, her lids closing. God, I'm drunk, she thought.

"Because you're beautiful. And you're young," Jeannette said. "Martin's forty-five. All he has is his money and his job." And they all looked at her oddly. What was she talking about?

"Are you kidding?" Erica said, "I'm the one with nothing. He's got everything. I've been sitting there, and he's been doing all the doing for seventeen years. I've got nothing, Jeannette."

Jeannette looked at her. "Now, maybe you've got nothing. But wait a year. Martin loses in the long run. That's what I know." She sat back then smoking, and the rest of them fell silent.

"How's your nineteen-year-old?" Sue asked, ordering another beer.

"Good," she said.

"You don't want to talk about it?"

"No. Not tonight," Jeannette said.

"Why not?" Elaine asked. "Are we hateful tonight? Is it like the gathering of the witches?"

Jeannette didn't smile. "Close to it."

"I'm going home," Erica said. "It's late." She got up then, feeling very drunk, more than she had anticipated, and walked down the length of the bar. She felt rotten. The man who had said hello when she walked in was still there. He was watching her. He followed her and held open the door. Then he hailed her a cab.

"Get lost," she said. "I can hail my own cab." He hailed it, anyway, opened the door, put her inside, and closed the door. Was he being nice? she wondered. She gave the driver the address and saw the man reach in the window and give the driver three dollars.

She rolled down the window as the cab started to pull away. "I have money," she said. "I have money, my own money." She broke into tears as she said it, and he looked at her as the cab pulled away, and then slowly, dreamily, he blew her a kiss.

6

ERICA FIRST DECIDED she needed a shrink when she fell in love with the man who blew her a kiss, and went back to look for him. He wasn't there. A week after that, she again decided she needed a shrink when she couldn't pay attention to anything anyone was saying. A kind of staggering impatience consumed her, no one talked fast enough, no one did anything fast enough, no one got to the point fast enough. The point, anything other than the point, assaulted her with its irrelevancy. What was the matter? Why was everyone so slow?

The third time someone told her she was rude, she began to notice it. She knew, of course, this gathering impatience for things to end—words, phrases, sentences, thoughts—was, in some convoluted, obsessed, and totally symbolic way, her own need to end her relationship with Martin. He had told her once she couldn't bear transitions. A thing was, or it wasn't, and now she realized fully what he meant. She couldn't bear this. She wanted, now, to be divorced tomorrow morning, to have it all over with, to never see him again.

See him. Have you "seen" Martin? they would all ask. They didn't mean "see," of course, as in "have you looked at." They meant, Is it straightened out? Is it clear? They, too, desperately wanted it to be clear. *They wanted to know what happened*. What happened. Somewhere Erica wanted to know, too.

"I decided to see a shrink," she told Patti at dinner that night.

"You decided that two weeks ago."

"Well, I decided it again."

"I think you should," Patti said tentatively. Some evenings Erica couldn't bear to look at her. It was evenings like this when there were just the two of them. God, it was lonely. Why was just Patti and Erica so lonely? Because she knew they were reminders to each other they had been left. But then, Sue and Elaine and Jeannette were all reminders, too, somehow. Oddly, Jeannette was the one she was most drawn to these days. Probably because Jeannette was in love, or thought she was, with that Steven. Actually, Erica liked him. He didn't look quite as bad as she expected. He looked young, but he could pass for twenty-four or twenty-five. He wasn't cute or boyish. And he was great with Jeannette. She was astounded how they were with each other.

"I think it's sick," Elaine had said to her on the phone.

"Well, I think it's rather nice," Erica said. "You forget how young he is when you're there. I mean, sort of. I mean, he doesn't act like a kid."

"It's still sick."

"I think it's good," Erica said defensively.

"Look, I never said sick wasn't also good," Elaine said. "Sick is usually sick. But sometimes sick is good until, of course, it gets sick again."

"I think you're losing your mind."

"Maybe my mind, but never my sexuality. You been laid yet?"

"I thought you were my friend."

"I am your friend, Erica. But you're scared. And you won't admit it. You're frightened shitless. You've got to get to a shrink. You won't see Martin. You won't call a lawyer. You won't get laid, and you don't drink. I mean, you may as well be dead."

Erica laughed, despite herself. "O.K., I'll do it." That had been a week ago. Jeannette had gotten her a doctor's name, but Erica had lost it. Then someone in the gallery, one of Veronique's friends, was talking about a woman shrink who changed her life. Erica had overheard the conversation and heard the name. She knew the office was only a few blocks from her home. The path of least resistance.

"I want you to, Mom." It was Patti's voice. Had Patti been talking while Erica was thinking?

"Want me to what?"

"Go to the shrink."

"Why do you want me to go?"

"Because you tell me too much. You keep telling me things about how you feel. I don't want to know." The eyes that met Erica's were cold. Don't do this to me, they said. I don't want to worry about you. I want to worry about me.

That was Patti. Straight, tough, and confident.

"I'm going to call this woman in the morning."

"Why don't you call her now?"

"Because it's after five o'clock," Erica said, irritated.

"They all live in their houses, Mom. I think shrinks take calls at seven. Anyway, you could leave a message with her service."

"What makes you think she has a service?" Erica suddenly felt trapped.

"They all do."

"How do you know so much about shrinks?"

"Phil had one."

"Phil did?" Erica gulped. Why did Phil need one? Was he a secret murderer? she wondered. "How come?"

"He felt lousy all the time after his brother had gotten killed. Too lousy for the famous 'time heals all wounds' cure. So after three years, when he kept flunking, they bought him a shrink as a Christmas present."

"Does he still go?"

"Yeah."

"Did it help him?"

"He said so. He stopped flunking. And he doesn't feel lousy. He said I should go."

"YOU?" Erica was taken aback. "Patti, you are the last person in the world that needs a shrink."

"Phil said you would say that."

"Patti, you and Phil are getting a little too smart-ass, a little too wise-ass for my taste. Phil said I would say that. What am I, subject for study, suddenly?"

"No. But Phil said you wouldn't let me go because you have to think I'm so perfect all the time!" Patti was angry. "Well, I'm not perfect, and I'm sick and tired of hating you all the time. I hate you a lot!" She screamed at Erica now and ran into the other room.

"Oh Jesus Christ!" Erica slammed her fist on the table, the dishes jumped, and she grabbed her coat and went for a walk.

As she walked down the stairs, she thought, I've never walked out on Patti. I never have. Well, it's too bad. She went to the street and walked three blocks. She knew the shrink's address. She walked past the building, and then around the block again. Then she went home. When she got into the house, it was very quiet.

"Patti?"

"I'm upstairs."

"What are you doing?"

"I'm calling Phil!"

Phil. Oh, God. Phil. He's more important to her than I am. Well, was that so terrible? Hanging up her coat, she thought it was probably not so terrible, but it made her feel terrible. In any event, Patti was right. Erica dialed the shrink's number. To her dismay, a voice answered on the second ring.

"Uh, hello?" Erica said, "I must have the wrong number."

"What number did you want?"

"Oh, uh," Erica looked at a piece of paper.

"Dr. Berkel."

"This is Dr. Berkel," said a faintly accented voice.

"Oh. Well, I was calling—I'm sorry to bother you at this hour. Do you want me to call back tomorrow?"

"It is no bother. Did you wish an appointment?"

Got straight to the point. Obviously.

"Er, uh, yes. My name is Erica Benton and I, uh, my husband left me."

"Tomorrow I am free at ten A.M.," the voice said.

"Tomorrow?" Erica said, startled. "I wasn't thinking about tomorrow. I was thinking about next week."

"You cannot come tomorrow?" the voice asked.

"Oh, no, I can come, I—" Erica felt suddenly like a total idiot. "I'll see you at ten tomorrow," she said, feeling suddenly defeated.

"Good."

"Good-bye," Erica said, and hung up. She felt defeated and angry. What was she, some kind of wreck she needed a shrink? She hated the idea of shrinks, she really did. She hated the idea a lot. Elaine had had one, and Sue, and Jeannette. But not Erica. She had been proud of the fact.

When Erica entered the shrink's office, the first thing she said was, "I want to make it perfectly clear I am here for this one visit in order to accommodate my daughter. I am not coming back. I am only coming here for this one time."

At the end of the hour, she agreed to come back again the next day. At the end of the week, she was beginning to admit it was making her feel better. But other than to Patti she absolutely couldn't get herself to admit it to anyone. Not even Elaine.

But the end of the second week, Tanya, which was what Dr. Berkel preferred to be called, said to Erica, "I do not tell people what to do. That is what you want me to do. But I have a fee. I must be paid. You tell me you must discuss this with Martin, but you also refuse to see Martin. You must realize the complexity of this. We must talk about it."

Erica snapped at her, "Is that all you want, Tanya, money?" And was immediately sorry.

"If I do this for nothing," Tanya said, smiling softly, "there is no cure."

Erica knew this to be true, but it bothered her, anyway. "I guess I have to talk about seeing Martin." She paused. "I hate the idea of seeing him. He reminds me I'm alone. Left. Without a man. Everywhere I go I see couples. Holding hands, arms around waists, cheek-to-cheekers. I hate it. I feel cold. My bed feels cold. I still tell Patti too much. I think you helped her, Tanya." Erica looked up. "She's very strong, that girl. Very. Martin called her yesterday, and he's going to see her. She's happy. . . . I'm glad, I think, about her leaving home, going off to college, getting married. It's a couple of years away, but I think about it as if it's going to happen tomorrow."

"It's not abnormal to think about it," Tanya said.

"I guess I'm lonely."

"I was lonely, too, when I was divorced."

"I didn't know you were divorced."

"Now you know. There's nothing wrong with feeling lonely. Or depressed. Or angry. Or anything. They're feelings. Sometimes I feel good, sometimes I feel lousy. But I'm not ashamed of how I feel."

"I feel guilty about it."

"You forget they're your feelings. You're entitled to them."

"When were you divorced?" Erica looked at the woman. She didn't have a divorced look, Erica thought. Whatever that was.

"Three years ago. Did you feel this lonely when you were married?" Tanya asked.

"Not much. I don't think so." Erica shifted uncomfortably. "I needed to be alone a lot. Martin didn't. He wanted to be with people all the time. But men are different. They don't need to be alone the way women do, do you think?"

"I think there are individual differences," Tanya said. "Did you want to be alone a lot?"

"Not a lot. But I liked it. I mean, I wasn't scared then. This scares me. Then I knew it wasn't going to mean I was going to be alone forever."

"You think you're going to be alone forever?"

"Well, at the rate I'm going . . . I mean, I think about it. I haven't, you know, been with a man for eight weeks now. I always took sex for granted. I'm beginning to feel that, all right." Erica looked up at Tanya. "I wish you'd say something." Then she looked at the floor. "This isn't much fun, this conversation," Erica said, toeing the rug. "Where was I?"

"Sex," Tanya said.

Erica laughed. "I was hoping you'd forgotten . . . you know, I've always thought of myself as being well adjusted sexually."

"I don't know what that means."

"I had a good sex life. I wasn't embarrassed about sex. I took it for granted. It was fun. We were pretty wild, Martin and I. . . ."

"I don't know what that means, either," Tanya said.

Erica felt on the spot. She was suddenly angry, and she spun around and yelled at Tanya, "It means we fucked and we sucked. Now do you know what it means?"

"Why are you so angry?" Tanya asked, leaning back and lighting a cigarette. Suddenly Erica wanted to punch her.

"Why am I so angry, right? What have I got to be angry about? Is that what you're asking?" Tanya said nothing. "Oh, I suppose it's because you know I am thinking, or rather I am feeling like seeing other men and it's scary, and I feel like I don't know how to do it, and I guess I'm asking you what to do. I mean, I seem to have a lot of French perfume ads running through my brain. Like that night I went back to the bar wanting to see Mr. Wonderful. And he wasn't there. I thought later, What the hell would I have done if he was there? Walked in and said, 'Hi, can I buy you a drink?' Well," Erica said impatiently, "say something."

"I can't tell you what to do. You know that."

"I know," Erica said. "I wish you could, though."

"I know what I would do, though," Tanya said, looking at Erica carefully.

"What?" Erica asked, surprised.

"I would go out and get laid."

Erica laughed. "Oh, God, it's like being a virgin all over again," she said. But she knew it wasn't. She left Tanya's feeling peculiar. She knew some kind of bargain had been struck. She had been looking for permission. And Tanya had given it. Whose permission did she want? Martin's? Walking down Third Avenue, Erica began to laugh. "I think I should call him up and ask him if it's O.K." The idea delighted her. Absolutely delighted her.

When she got home she called Elaine. "How are you?" Erica said, still amused.

"I thought you'd never ask. You certainly are keeping a low profile lately."

"I've been seeing a shrink."

"Uninterruptedly for two weeks? He must be good."

"It's a she."

"Does she help?"

"I think so. She makes me feel better, anyway."

"When are we going to get together?"

"Soon. Maybe next week for dinner."

"Are you free tonight?" Elaine said. "I have someone coming over you'd like."

"A man?"

"Natch."

"No," Erica said, "I can't tonight."

"You have a date?"

"Sort of," Erica said.

"Oh, I get it," Elaine said. "You're going to a bar."

Erica burst out laughing. "Elaine! I didn't say that."

"But you are."

"I'll call you next week," Erica said, smiling. And hung up. You bet your ass I am, she said, to absolutely no one in particular.

She arranged her plans for the evening like an army general. First there was Patti.

"Patti, are you going out tonight?"

"No, Mom. I have too much to do."

"Well, you don't mind if I do, do you?"

"It'd be a relief, frankly. I mean"—Patti smiled—"don't take it personally."

"Oh," Erica said, "I wouldn't dream of taking it personally. Well, look, I'm going to be late, I think. I mean, I may not be, but more probably I will be late, quite late. So don't get upset if you don't find me home until late."

"Are you trying to tell me you're sleeping with someone?"

"I am not," Erica said evenly, "trying to tell you anything other than what I am trying to tell you. I'm going to a party, and I think it's going to get late. Quite late. Very late, in fact. So I don't know if I'll stay for the whole thing, but if I do, it'll be late."

"O.K.," Patti said calmly. "I'm taking a bath. See you tomorrow morning," and she went upstairs.

Erica took her time getting dressed, applying the makeup. Now she knew what it was all about, playing hunter. She knew she was going to Springs, a SoHo bar where most of the artists hung out. That would be her declaration. She had not been keeping very good hours at the gallery, and she had not really felt like having a discussion about her life with any of them, so Herb really was the only one she knew. Tanya had said it seemed as if she had a dirty secret. And it was like that. In a way. Well, tonight was the coming-out party. And she looked it. Erica pulled out a brand-new pair of burgundy-colored boots, attached her silver collar bracelet, her cashmere brandy-colored cowl, got into her tightest jeans, stuffed them into the boots, and took a final check of her makeup.

"Not bad," she said. "You might have a future, after all." Every once in a while it would catch her, what would she have done if she wasn't good-looking? It meant she felt so ugly being good-looking, if you were really ugly and felt ugly, it could only be worse. Actually Erica had never thought she felt bad about herself, other than those bad days. But it was true that when she was married to Martin she had often felt that parties were an agony, not because she wasn't good conversationally; she always had that sinking sensation that no one would ever want to talk to her. And often, they didn't.

She had said to Elaine once, "What do I do wrong?"

"It's something about your expression. You turn people off. I don't know what the hell it is. You act like you don't want them to talk to you."

"I do, though," Erica had said. But then she wondered if she did after all. She got bored so easily. So easily. Usually she thought about it now when men were talking to her. She found her interest would drop off mid-conversation. Once, a man had said to her, "I can see you don't find me very interesting after all. I can tell by the expression on your face. Sorry I bored you," and he turned and left her. She wanted to call after him and apologize. But it was the truth. Elaine was funny that way. Just the opposite. At a party she was a three-hundred-watt glow. Talking, chatting, amusing, entertaining everyone, finding everything funny, interesting, intense. Even Jeannette, normally quiet, would find one or two people and spend the evening talking. Erica roamed the room like a cat, lighting a few minutes here, a few more minutes there. It had bothered her for years, and then she forgot about it. She and Martin went to fewer and fewer parties together. He would go alone, and he kept those to a minimum.

Maybe, Erica thought, getting into her coat, I really was a hostile little bitch all along. Well, we'll find out tonight.

Patti came downstairs just as she was leaving.

"Oh, wow, do you look good," Patti said, her face lighting up.

"Thanks. Do I smell good, too?" Erica had doused herself with something that smelled good.

"Yeah. You never wear perfume."

"Now I wear perfume," Erica said, and Patti smiled, kissed her good-bye, and said, "Have a good time."

Erica felt the sharp pang of role reversal. She felt like sixteen again.

When Erica got to the bar, she was relieved to see it was crowded. That made it all easier somehow. She made her way through the crowd, took a seat, and ordered a Chablis. A very attractive man came toward her, smiling. This is it, she thought. He leaned past her to the bartender and said, "Two beers, Tommy." Then Erica saw the woman leaning against the post waiting for him. That was not it, then. She took a few more sips from her glass, and then, feeling silly, she got up and walked to the back of the room. She saw Jean Evans, a painter who had made quite a reputation in Paris and was now back in the States. She was black, and an American, and very attractive. She was with a man Erica didn't know.

"Hi, Erica. I haven't seen you around in a while. You're looking really good."

"Thanks. Hi, Jean."

"This is Edward Theroux, he just got back from Europe," Jean said. "Erica works at the Rowan."

"Hi. I hear the new show is quite something."

"It's very controversial," Erica said. "Either you hate it or you love it."

"Edward just got back from a year in Rome. He's a painter, too."

"How was Rome?" Erica asked, feeling stupid.

"Frankly," he smiled, "it's very controversial. You either hate it or you love it. I loved it."

"What's happening with you, Erica?" Jean asked.

"Well, frankly, I'm a little weird these days. I'm getting a divorce," Erica said. There. Not so bad. Out.

"Oh, I'm surprised," Jean said, looking it.

"Everybody is. Why are you?"

"Oh, I guess you seem like such a normal type. Compared to me, that is."

"It's all the normal people getting divorced. The rest of the pack doesn't even bother getting married."

"If I'd gotten married every time I thought it was *serious*," Jean said, starting to laugh, "I'd be in Zsa Zsa Gabor's league. . . ."

"How's your life?" Erica asked.

"Well, I'm sculpting pretty good now, trying my

hand at that, and Edward and I are definitely an item."

"See that? I've been nothing but nice to her, and
hand at that, and Edward and I are definitely an item."
already she's calling me an item."

Suddenly Erica spotted Charlie making a beeline toward them. Charlie didn't know anything about Erica's divorce yet.

"Hi, Erica," he said, looking pleased to see her. "Are you slumming?"

"I wasn't up to now," she said. She said it before she could stop it.

But Charlie, to her surprise, didn't get defensive. He turned to Jean. "What does she want from me? This girl beats on me all the time. Hi," he said, turning to Edward.

They shook hands, and Jean said, "There's a party at Tom Whalen's loft. Why don't you come?"

"Whalen?" Charlie said, "the guy who paints turtles?"

"Yeah."

"I pass."

"You want to come, Erica?" Jean said, putting her beer down on the bar.

"Thanks, Jean. I don't think so. It was nice to meet you," she said to Edward.

"*Arrivederla*," he said, in a good enough accent to get away with it. Although Charlie evidently didn't think so.

"*Arrivederla*, my ass," Charlie mumbled.

"Is prejudice another one of your charming traits, Charlie?" Erica asked.

"What are you doing here alone?" he asked, ignoring the question. "Where's 'darling'?"

"We're getting divorced." Actually Erica enjoyed saying it.

"Sure."

"Charlie, it's true. He left me for a schoolteacher.

She was buying a shirt in Bloomingdale's, and he fell in love."

"Is that too much?" Charlie's face was shocked.

"For me it was."

"Hey, should I be worried?" he said.

"No."

"Wow."

"Yeah, wow. Buy me another glass of wine."

"Be right back." Charlie turned and headed for the bar. When he returned, he saw Erica's face was tight.

"What's the matter?"

"Nothing's the matter. What's the matter with you?"

"Nothing's the matter with me. You look like something's the matter."

"Charlie, you once said you could tell everything about a woman by her eyes. Look in my eyes. What do you see?"

Charlie stared at her. "I see fear, confusion."

"Wrong. See anything else?"

"I don't know." He looked at her. "There's something else there. I'm not sure what it is."

Erica drank the glass of wine in one gulp. "Take me to your loft, Charlie. I'll show you what else is there."

Erica had to keep from laughing at the look on his face. He fumbled with the money for the bartender, he fumbled getting his coat on, her coat on, but somehow they were out the door. Erica knew his loft was less than a block away, so she was amused, and relieved by his sudden, compulsive volubility.

"Look, my loft, you know I been redoing the floors, and I put new sashes in so I could get a different kind of glass, you know it doesn't do anything funny to the light at all, 'course it's a freight elevator and the freight elevator doesn't always work, so sometimes we have to use the stairs, that's a killer, I mean, eight flights of stairs is a killer."

"Eight flights?" Erica stopped walking.

"Yeah, but don't worry, the elevator almost always works. C'mon." He pulled her arm.

I must be out of my mind, she thought. Why this son of a bitch of all people? A pathetic son of a bitch. Still, something in her warmed toward him. She knew why it was Charlie. She wasn't afraid of him.

When they got into the loft, Charlie seemed to be in a nervous twit. I thought I was bad, Erica thought. First he asked her if she wanted coffee. Then he asked her if she wanted wine, and went foraging into his cupboard for wine, which she didn't want. Finally, she said, "Charlie, let's do it now. Before I change my mind," and she started to take her clothes off. To her amazement, Charlie started a lecture.

"Look, Erica, I'll tell you now. I don't get involved with my women. I'm a short-term guy. I don't believe in marriage. I don't fall in love. You can't count on me for anything but sex. I am what I am, and I don't make any bones about it."

"Charlie"—Erica had taken her sweater and pants off and now stopped—"I am very nervous. All your talking is making me more nervous. I don't want to marry you. I just want to get into bed. Now hurry up."

He shut up then and looked at her. She stood there waiting for him to get undressed, and he went to the bed and hurled off his boots, his shirt, and his pants in a minute. He didn't wear underclothes. She should have known.

"Well, come on," he said looking at her. She turned and shut off the lights. Then she took her bra and pants off. "Where the hell are you?" he said. "I can't see."

"That was the idea."

"You act like some kind of virgin."

"Charlie, I've only slept with one man in seventeen years."

"I was wrong about you. I could have sworn you'd

had a few affairs. Where are you?" Suddenly she felt hi
arms on her, and then around her. He moved mor
softly than she thought; he pulled her down beside him
"Jesus, you have a beautiful body," he said, kissin
her shoulder. "You're shaking," he said. He didn't tr
to pull her closer, but began kissing her back, down he
back.

"Charlie?"

"What?"

"I think I'm lying on a tube of paint." She sounde
plaintive.

"I'll lick it off. Relax," he said, holding her.

Erica lay still against Charlie for a moment, he
heart pounding, as he stroked her back, her thigh, an
kissed her shoulder. She was grateful he took a lon
time loving her. She felt herself giving in to it. Sh
thought she didn't like him. But she liked this part o
him. She knew she liked him more than she thought, o
should, that it was no accident that it was Charlie sh
was in bed with, that the feel, the build, the heat of hi
body next to her all excited her more than she'd expected. She loved the smell of him in the dark, the smel
of a man, and that man, but a definite smell, the hars
sweep of his beard moving over her, his arms stron
around her, the flesh of his hips, his hands; he wa
taking a long time with her, moving around her like a
snake, kissing her toes, her knees, her hips, moving t
her belly until her legs opened, and then he moved int
her like a locomotive, charging her so strongly sh
gasped, and then taking a long, full time, feeling he
peak, letting her down, letting her peak again, an
stroking and kissing her until she felt herself unfold, unfold, and still wanting him more, she had not felt tha
kind of fevered desire before; she put her hands on hi
hips, her legs were way over her head, and pulled him
hard into her, as deep as he could go, and then he roare
and came gloriously collapsing over her. He engulfed he

that night. She gave herself completely, utterly to him and he knew it. He savored it. And when she got up to get dressed, late—she guessed it must be about five or six —he caught her softly and said, "Hey, you can't go, not after that, you can't go," and she kissed him again then, lovingly and longingly, and said, "I have to." She didn't want to stay. She felt, even dressing, the startling compromise of her condition. Sexually she had wanted him, terribly so. She had felt such desire that she had bitten her tongue rather than scream, I love you, I love you, but that moment, in that bed, she had loved him. And she had not intended to. Not Charlie. She had chosen Charlie as the target of a good balling. And he had encompassed her, wanted her so, he had moved her into the center of her own desire. She had surrendered until she was weak. She had never felt anything like it in her life. It now seemed to her the most important thing in her entire life was to get out of his apartment, away from him, quickly, unless she disappear into some warm washed world of feeling away from thinking, too far away from herself to be comfortable.

"I'll see you tonight," he said definitely, lying on the bed.

"You're beautiful," she said to him smiling, "and I like your paintings a lot."

"I like you." He got up and held her. Then he kissed her. She did like his kissing her. She had needed him last night, and he knew it, and didn't exploit it, he knew it and reveled in it, and she had been completely, totally his. Charlie. Of all people. She shook her head in amazement.

"What are you shaking your head about?"

"Life. Life forces."

"What are those?"

"My daughter's boyfriend knows. You have to ask him. I have to go home now. I want to be home for breakfast."

"I'll see you tonight," he said, leaning back, confident.

"No, you won't," she said, getting on her coat.

"Are you mad about something?"

"No."

"Then come back tonight."

"No, I said no."

"Why not?"

"Because," she turned to him smiling, "I'm a short-term girl. Don't get involved with me, Charlie. You'll only get hurt. I don't believe in marriage. I don't fall in love, I travel a lot." He began to laugh then, and blush.

"I'm on the road all the time," she said slowly.

"I'll tell you one thing," he said, getting up and grabbing her. "Your old man is an asshole."

"Good night, Charlie." She kissed him for a long time, and then was out the door.

She called Martin that morning and told him she wanted to see him. He seemed overjoyed to hear from her and told her to come to the office. Erica had never been to his office before. It was impressive. He was on the twenty-eighth floor.

When she saw him, she thought he looked like a total stranger. He greeted her warmly. "Hi, come in. Gee, you look really great. Really good. Have a seat. Sit down." He was nervous. Then he closed the door.

"So tell me," he said, sitting back in his chair. "What's new?"

"I got laid last night," Erica said. It was one of her best moments. She sat there savoring the expression on Martin's face. He turned pale.

"Look, Erica, did you come here to talk, or did you come here to break balls?"

"I came to break balls," she said calmly.

"Well, then, get out." He stood and yelled, "GET OUT!" and opened the door.

"I'm not done yet. Patti needs money."

"Oh, Patti does. What about you? You living on love alone?"

"Patti's seeing a therapist. So am I. Patti's very angry at you. The therapist is helping. It's expensive."

"Tell her to send me the bills. For the lot of you." He sat down again. "What's the therapist's name?"

"Tanya Berkel."

"A woman?"

"I never heard of a man named Tanya."

"Good."

"I'm glad you think it's good."

Martin leaned forward. "You really hate me, don't you?"

"Yeah."

"I don't hate you," Martin said.

"You always were a compassionate man."

How the hell can you hate someone you were in love with for seventeen years? He was standing up and stalking around the room. "How can love turn to hate so fast, would you tell me that?"

"It's easy."

"If you want to make me feel any guiltier than I do, you're succeeding."

"Good."

"This is ridiculous, Erica. What do you want?"

"Martin, do you know how many times we had sex?"

"I'd rather not talk about it."

"At least two thousand times. That's figuring twice a week for seventeen years. Put it up on your ticker tape."

"There were weeks when we . . . when it was four or five," he smiled. The male ego, Erica thought, always reigns supreme.

"Martin, I've had it with you." Erica got up.

"Where are you going?"

"I am going out, where do you think? I'm not staying."

"What did you have to see me about?" He was pleading with her to stay.

"I'll see you another time. I don't want to talk about it now," and she slammed the door. Bastard. Bragging about it. I suppose he does it with her nine times a week. I suppose they fuck like there's no tomorrow—and me, what did I do? Just lay there, looking at the ceiling. Bastard. A man was coming through the door as Erica went out. She was walking fast and didn't see him and crashed right into him. He staggered backward and began to apologize, although it clearly wasn't his fault.

"OH, SHUT UP!" Erica screamed. "SHUT up, you stupid bastard. Shut the fuck up." And she strode off down the hall. The man stood there staring after her, murmuring, "Out of her mind, she's absolutely crazy," and then, bursting into the next room, said to the secretary, "Who was that woman?"

"Oh," the secretary turned to him, "that's Martin Benton's ex-wife."

"She's out of her goddamned mind."

"Yes, that's what Mr. Benton just said," the secretary said.

Erica knew that Charlie would come by the gallery soon. And she didn't want to see him. She absolutely didn't want to see him.

"Look, you don't have to see him," Elaine said, "in the sense of see him. But you tell me you go to bed with a guy and he blows you right off the sheets. I don't get it. I mean, you don't even want to have a cup of coffee with him? You don't want him again?"

"No, I don't want him again. I wanted him then. Once, finished, that was it. I mean, I'm free to do that, aren't I? Why do I have to owe him anything?"

"You don't," Elaine said. "But if it was anything like

you said for him, he'll be back. You won't get out of it that easily."

"Why should it matter to him? He's not madly in love with me."

"When guys know they turn you on like that, they can't let you go. You'll see."

"I don't get it myself, Elaine, that night I swear I thought I was madly in love with him. I loved being with him. It was incredible. And I don't even think I like him."

"You don't even like him?"

"Well, I like him, I think. But there's a lot about it I don't like. I mean, he's a real macho type. I mean, he's different in bed. He's very real in bed. With his clothes on, he's a real pain in the ass."

"You could get married and live in a nudist colony."

"Your ratings are falling," Erica said.

"Yeah, I know. Well. Good luck. See you next week."

"So long." Erica hung up, strangely unsatisfied. She didn't know what she expected, really. Did she think Elaine was going to solve everything, miraculously, for her? She felt guilty about Charlie, that was a fact. Guilty that she didn't want him at all.

"Tanya, it's crazy. Some man three weeks ago in a bar walks me out the door, hails me a cab, and blows me a kiss, and I am feeling that I hate men—all men, right—and he does that, and I go back to the bar the next night looking for him. I think I'm in love suddenly. He wasn't there."

"You told me about this."

"Well, it doesn't make any sense. I fall in love like that, I think, and then this thing with Charlie. I mean, I don't really like Charlie, and in bed I lost my mind.

There was so much I was putting into it, and he doesn't matter that much. I can take him or leave him."

"Maybe that has something to do with it," Tanya said.

"If that's it, I find it very depressing."

"That may be part of it right now. You're still very angry. You're so angry you may be able to feel uninhibited only with someone who isn't that important to you."

"Well, I do want to see him again. In a way. I mean, I don't want to talk to him. I don't want to have anything to do with him. I want to go to his apartment and I want him to make love to me like that and then I want to get up, get dressed, and get out." Erica paused for a moment. "I thought only men thought like that."

"People who are afraid of getting hurt. People who don't want connections talk like that."

"Do I have to want a connection?" Erica said angrily. "I'm sick of connections. I'm sick of it. I just want to be left alone!"

"It sounds like you're arranging that."

Charlie was waiting for her when she got to the gallery. He greeted her excitedly and then reached over to kiss her. She pulled away.

"It was only one night, Charlie. You don't own me." Her voice was hard. He pulled back, surprised.

"I don't want to own you," he said. His manner was different. He was softer with her. "I'd just like to ask you to dinner."

She was awful to him. She was difficult. Petulant. She said to call her later. He called her later. She relented and agreed to dinner. Throughout dinner he was so nice to her, so easy, so undefensive, so eager to please her she thought she was going to die. He was falling in love with her. He was smitten, utterly. She felt it. And then she had contempt for it. The ass. The fool. She hated him for loving her, in the same way she had been moved by it when they made love. It had been Charlie's wanting her so, he treated her like she was a prize, the crown jewels, he was so excited by her in his bed that he turned her on like she had never been turned on in her life. And now she couldn't stand him.

"It is what you hate in yourself. Your dependence, your devotion to Martin. You have contempt with yourself for loving him," Tanya said. "There is no need for that."

"I hurt Charlie, you know. I really killed him when I said I didn't want to see him again. I mean, he must really have had this crush on me. And now he knows I used him." Erica shuddered. "You should have seen his eyes when I told him after dinner I wouldn't see him anymore. There was sheer murder in them."

"He sounds like a man who does not give himself easily to women. And when he does, he gets hurt. He probably turns on to unavailable types."

"Am I unavailable?"

"What do you think, emotionally?"

"I'm unavailable," Erica shrugged. Unavailable and in need, she thought. She needed a man. She needed a man she wanted, she knew that. It had been only a week after the Charlie adventure that Erica had gone to a bar determined to pick up the most attractive man in it. Sheer looks. She did it, and when she found herself in his apartment, she realized the full weight of her error. She didn't want any part of it, but she was already in it. She went to bed with him like a stone, hating it. Hating what she had done to herself to get there. He was an idiot. A good-looking idiot. She left at 2:00 A.M. She had never given him her real name. Thank God. She was humiliated, angry, and disgusted with herself. The poor bastard, she thought, he thinks he's made a connection. He had gotten possessive about her leaving to the point where she really had to be emphatic. She gave him a false phone number and false last name, and left him, feeling like a whore.

7

THE NIGHT SHE MET Elaine, Jeannette, and Sue, she told them that she thought she had always been normal sexually. Now she thought she was crazy. She loved men; she hated them. She wanted them to love her when she was in bed with them, she couldn't be in bed with them unless she liked them, but even when she liked them, she couldn't bear a continuation. But to go to bed with one she didn't like, that was a nightmare.

"My God, you sound like you were in bed with Frankenstein. I mean, if he was so good-looking, what could be so bad?" Elaine said wonderingly.

"I didn't like him. He was dumb. He was boring. I didn't care."

"You didn't like Charlie, either," Elaine said.

"Oh, I did, though. I mean, he was smart; in some way there was a kind of tension—he was on the other end of the balancing pole, you know—there was some kind of relatedness, and he wanted me."

"This gorgeous one sounds like he wanted you."

"Yeah, but he didn't know me. He wanted a blond with a good ass, you know?"

"Don't look at me," Elaine said. "I don't go for blonds."

They all laughed, drinking, thoughtful, trying to put it together, not knowing what it was they were trying to put together, knowing somehow they were all in the same boat, and not in the same boat at all. But now

Erica knew that in a way she had been hiding in her marriage. Maybe it was the reason that people got married. It gave you this semblance of normalcy. If you were married, you couldn't be mixed up. It meant you were straight. Not confused. If you weren't married, it meant you were confused, if you were a woman. If you were a man, it just meant you didn't want to get married. Erica realized that in a way for a woman to get married was to strike a public-relations deal with the world. "I'm all right." I must be all right. I'm married. But not only with the world. With one's self. Now the full rush of the unsolved confrontations within her was upon her. She didn't think she liked it. If it weren't for Tanya, she knew she wouldn't think about it at all. Socrates said the unexamined life was not worth living. Well, she had news for Socrates. The unexamined life was a relief, in a way. She had liked not having to examine it. Now everything seemed full of contradiction—loving people, hating people, good sex, bad sex, wanting, not wanting, connecting, not connecting, dependence, separateness, communion—and in the midst of those thoughts, she would think of Charlie, some sense of his masculinity would overwhelm her, and she would want him again.

"He reeks masculinity," Elaine had said, having spotted Charlie on the street and then followed him to a bar.

"How do you know?" Erica had said.

"When you pointed him out to me, after I left you, I followed him to a bar."

"You did?" Erica felt oddly threatened.

"Yeah. I tried to pick him up."

"What happened?"

"He couldn't have been less interested."

"So what'd you think?"

"He's sexy," Elaine said, "but a real pain in the ass.

Still, there's something appealing about him. If he'd only take off those leather wrist bands."

And so it had gone. The next few weeks had plunged Erica into a confusion she found totally bewildering. Wanting, not wanting. And then, after two weeks of not seeing Charlie, she was hot. Really hot. And hot for him. She called him up.

"Hi, Charlie."

"Who's this?"

"Erica."

She knew he knew who it was.

"I thought you were dead."

"Wishful thinking?"

"Maybe." He was relenting, even over the phone. "What do you want?"

That's right, Charlie, don't give me any room. Don't leave me an inch.

Erica took a breath. "I thought you might want to go out for a drink."

"When, now?"

"Yeah."

"I'm working. I'm all messed up. I mean, you're a killer, Erica. You tell me you don't ever want to see me again, and then you call me up just like that and want to have a drink. What the hell is it—you want me to ball you, is that it? You got hot and you want to come over and ball me!" He was furious.

"Charlie, I want to come over and ball you," she said evenly.

"Well, fuck you!" He hung up.

She waited. In ten minutes the phone rang.

"Hi," she said.

"Come over," he said. And she did.

It was insane. It was as insane as anything else, Erica realized. She hated going to his building. She hated going up in the elevator to the loft. She hated ringing the bell. When he answered it, she even hated it. She hated their standing there looking at each other.

"Are you going to ask me in, or do I stand in the hall?"

There, that brittleness again, the brittleness he brought out in her.

"Get your ass in here," he said, looking at her. Then he poured her some wine.

"I don't want any wine." She felt wild suddenly, caged. She wanted out of there.

"Have the wine," he said evenly, pulling out a chair.

"I don't want it," she said.

"I need you to have it," he said, and she nearly died. To save his face. Oh, God. But she wanted him. Wasn't that something?

"Charlie, if you want me to go, I'll go. It's not any different. I don't want any connections, to anything. I know I'm bitchy to you. I know I am." She sighed and looked at him. "But I want to go to bed with you."

He turned to her then, and turned away. He walked to the wall and turned off the light.

"Get your clothes off," he said. And she put the wine down, and undressed, and stood by the edge of the bed. And then he got up and turned the light on.

"What are you doing?" She was suddenly awkward.

"I want to see you," he said. And it was too much for her. She didn't want him seeing her, even. She just wanted him in the dark.

"Turn it off," she said. And he surprised her then because he came over and grabbed her, and she was hard, resistant, and then gave in to him, God, he knew how to kiss her. And then he put her on the bed and stroked her and she said, "Turn the lights off," and he said, "No." And he made love to her and she melted into him, she had never wanted a man like that before, wanted him deep inside, desperate for him to stay inside, inside, the sense of him surrounding her, the smell of him deep in his neck, his hair scratching her face, and his weight. There was something magic in his weight on her, leaning into her, and yet she could manage it, she was flexible moving under him, and they were together, as rhythmic as could be, she had never known that beat with Martin, now with Charlie, he was a man, whatever it meant, all man, he was that to her, in his smell and his weight and his desperate wanting of her. "You're killing me, baby," he said to her as he loved her and she knew she was, she knew he was in an agony for her and it turned her on fiercely and she gave him everything again, gave him everything because he couldn't take it finally because finally she owed him nothing, because finally she didn't love him and could give herself to him then, unowned, unpossessed, free, wild and full of desire, she wanted him in a terrible, ferocious, unfettered way. He felt it and loved it and took it and it was hours later and they were still sweating and they slept with the lights on, glistening.

And when she got up and got dressed, he wouldn't look at her. He lay on his back smoking a cigarette. In bed, naked, all sex, Charlie had a kind of perfection that astounded her. She looked at him and she loved him, if that was love. To look. He was beautiful. In his need, his wanting, his loving, he was beautiful. And he said nothing as she got dressed, and she felt cheap. He just smoked quietly, and then he said, "You're killing me. Nobody ever did that before." And she finished dressing and kissed him on the eyes and said, "Charlie, I . . ." and that was all she could say. She wanted to tell him she loved him then, but in an hour, when the sun was up, she would hate him, she knew. Hate him then for loving her. And so she didn't say it, and opened the door and went out.

And then she cried. On the way home in the cab, she sobbed. What in the name of God she was crying about she didn't know.

8

"I DON'T GET IT, Tanya," Erica said to her therapist the next morning. "I'm freer in bed with Charlie than I ever was in my life, and I treat him like dirt. I like treating him like dirt. I want to go in there and make love and get out. When he shows up in the daytime, I could die. When he looks at me in the daytime, I could die."

"How does he look at you in the daytime?"

Erica looked at the floor. "With affection. Almost devotion. It makes me think of . . ." She stopped, ashamed.

"Of what?"

"Of a cocker spaniel I used to have." Then she burst out laughing. But it sounded desperate. She caught it, and Tanya caught it. "Oh, God, a cocker spaniel. I mean, he looks so *devoted*."

"Do you think he really looks like that?"

"What do you mean, do I really think he looks like that? Of course I think he looks like that—isn't that what I just said?"

"Does he look like that to anyone else or just to you?"

"You mean, am I projecting, am I putting something there that isn't there?"

"It seems you see either total dependence, a slavish dog, or someone you have nothing to do with. You don't have any middle ground right now."

"And you, Tanya?" Erica said suddenly, savagely angry, "are you so hot at working middle ground?"

"Why are you so angry?"

Erica stared at her. "I don't know."

Tanya didn't pursue it. Someone had told her Tanya was a lesbian, and Erica had first been shocked, and then disappointed. She couldn't bring herself to say it to Tanya. Erica was ashamed to admit her judgment about it. It diminished Tanya somehow, and yet she had helped Erica a lot. It was amazing, when she thought about it, that one afternoon a week could be so reassuring. But then Erica realized she had a long way to go. When a friend had told her that Martin was in "group," she had lashed out, "Group? Oh, that's unbelievable. At his age, yet. That horse's ass. That's the latest thing now. Group therapy. What a crock." She had been amazed at this hard edge in herself that emerged at times like that. Actually, all she felt was contempt for Martin for being in group, or looking for any kind of help. She felt he had been converted by the public exhibition of his need into an absolute idiot. And the idea of his sitting around in group discussing the details of his sex life or *their* sex life absolutely appalled her.

"I don't think they go into that kind of detail," Elaine had explained to her, rather nervously. "I mean, about who is good or not good in bed, you know."

"Elaine," Erica said tiredly, "I'm not worried about my reputation. It's my privacy. Remember that old thing?"

"You're getting bitchy."

"You always did bring out the best in me."

Elaine hung up. Erica swore to herself and decided that the time had come for her to confront Martin. Enough was enough. If only she could hold out. If only she could predict the way she would feel. There were days when she woke up like a tiger, feeling full of anger, but in a good solid way, days when she felt she could tell Martin off in two minutes, when she felt the supreme power of the "one who has been left," the power to evoke guilt, the power to remain the "good one," when she felt supremely confident because of that, and then there were other days when she felt weak, confused, and awful, days when she thought she would do anything in the world to have Martin take her back, "take her back," again, she thought, like a dog given up to the pound, to be "taken back," loved, cared for. Days when she thought about money. She could never face him on a day like that.

Yet she knew she had to free him, and she had to do something serious about the money issue. She not only had to hire a lawyer, but she had to think about what she, Erica, was going to do professionally. She had dabbled around at various things for years, but it had never seriously occurred to her that she had to support herself. Of course she didn't have to. Martin would be obligated to take care of that. Lawyers had assured her. But she wanted to, that was the thing. She didn't want to be hanging on Martin's income the rest of her life.

"I don't know why not," Sue said to her calmly that afternoon.

"What do you mean you don't know why not?" Erica had been surprised.

"Well, I mean, aren't you just a little bit vengeful?" Sue had said. "Frankly, it serves him right. I mean, if it's really final." She was shaking her head, pacing back and forth in Erica's kitchen. "And I must tell you I just can't believe it. I really can't." She threw up her hands. "But if you tell me it's final, and it's really final, then the hell with it. Make him pay for it."

"That's too easy," Erica had told her. "When he's paying for it, I'm paying for it. You know what I mean."

"Frankly, no," Sue said. "Besides, I'm sure he's coming back."

"What makes you think I want him back?" Erica was getting angry.

"Well, people always go for a second try. I mean, anything's better than being alone, and at first, you know, you don't think you can make it, so you'd probably take him back." Sue said this evenly, seated now on Erica's couch, taking long draws on her cigarette. Erica was getting furious, but she controlled it.

"You act like it's some sort of game. Like there are only so many moves, and statistically chances are that this will be the next move. I must say I'm surprised."

"There are only so many moves," Sue said quietly.

"Are things that rotten with you and Roger?" Erica said.

"No more than usual," Sue said.

"Why do you stand for it?"

Sue shrugged. "Look, he has to do what he has to do. I know he really loves me. And he always comes back."

"Is that it?" Erica said sharply, suddenly seeing the whole relationship in a new way.

"Is what it?"

"Is that why you put up with it, because he always comes back?"

"I don't know, Erica. You're beginning to sound like a therapist, so I'm leaving."

Sue stood up then, very unreachable, very composed, and, Erica thought, in a certain sense, a total stranger to her.

"Are you coming to the meeting tomorrow night?" Erica said suddenly, anxious at losing Sue's friendship, knowing that somehow in that moment she had.

Sue smiled. "I don't know. Depends on my mood."

"Look," Erica said, "I didn't mean to offend you. I can't understand you sometimes, that's all."

"I can't understand myself," Sue said in what was an uncharacteristically self-pitying way. "But you give up so much for a marriage. If they end it, I think you ought to kill them—at *least* at the bank. It's the only weapon women have," she said, looking at Erica. "You *have* to make him pay for it."

"I think you see it *all* as revenge," Erica said slowly. "I mean, don't think I wouldn't like to kill him. I would. I don't want his money, though." And then she felt a flare of anger. "And I didn't give up so much—only what I wanted to."

"That's what you think. You're a bigger ass than I thought," Sue said sharply, picking up her jacket. "You'll be holding onto your pride in your old age, and that's not enough."

"Look," Erica said hotly, "I'm thirty-six, not seventy-six, for chrissake. I can earn a living."

"Yeah," Sue said, "but you won't want to. You'll be looking for a man. And then when you find one, they take everything out of you—your independence, your motivation, everything." She stopped then, as if caught in a monologue, and said abruptly, "I'm just tired, Erica. Forget it."

Sue leaned over to kiss her good-bye, but Erica felt the sharp sense of separation that occurs in the discovery that someone isn't who you think after all. Sue was not a bright, funny girl with a difficult marriage. She was a bitter, vengeful woman tied to a man she thought had ruined her life.

After Sue left, Erica sat for a long time staring out the window. She felt physically ill, wondering, "Why does she stay? Why doesn't she leave him?" at the same time understanding that Sue wouldn't, that she couldn't.

9

THE MEETING of "the group," as they began to call themselves, had taken on a new importance with Erica's marital crisis, and Erica in a certain way enjoyed the sense that she was the star attraction, she was the one with the most potential, the most mobility in the group. As she got dressed for the meeting that night, she felt surprised that the old sense of her superiority among them had returned. Except for Jeannette. Jeannette did seem to have a new sense of herself, with this guy, that she didn't have before. Elaine was the only one who disagreed.

"Look, he's a kid," Elaine kept saying. "I just can't take him seriously."

"But he takes you seriously," Erica had said.

"What do you mean?"

"Well, you know he's not sexist, not at all. I mean, I never knew what the word meant until I saw the way he was with Jeannette."

"Oh, God, you mean serving dinner."

"That's not the whole thing. I mean the way he pays attention. And to other women. I mean, he likes women but he's—I don't know, he's different. He doesn't expect her to make the coffee."

"Big deal. I think he's weird."

"Why?"

"I hate to say it, but I think I like sexist men. Look,

I confuse easily. I need to know who's on top at all times."

Erica had laughed, but she thought there was more truth in it than she cared to know. Perhaps the most surprising thing about the change in her relationship with Martin was the changes that were taking place with her friends. She saw them differently now.

Erica was not surprised to find that Sue didn't show up at the restaurant that evening.

"I think I really got to her," Erica said, sitting down, noticing a very attractive man at the bar. She glanced his way again before she moved her chair into the table, and she was right. He was watching her.

"What'd you do?" Jeannette asked.

"I don't know," Erica said. "We were talking, you know, about Martin and Roger, and she kept saying he was coming back, and she made me feel like a martyr or something." Erica was moving her hands nervously. She didn't want to tell them what she really sensed about Sue. "I mean, just because Sue likes being married to somebody who screws around doesn't mean I have to."

Sue's voice was suddenly behind her. "I don't *like* it, Erica darling, hard as it may be for that dictatorial, pseudotherapy mind of yours to understand. I don't like it a bit. I think it's a rule of life."

Erica was embarrassed, and angry. "It's not a rule. I was married to Martin for years before he started screwing around." The minute she said it, she knew she shouldn't have.

Elaine again: "That's what you *think*. Not what you know."

"I know," Erica said, suddenly savage. And for some strange, queer reason, she knew she was right. She did know.

"If you knew he wasn't screwing around, you would

have known when he was screwing around. And you didn't," Elaine said calmly. "You said you hadn't a clue. You said he was the original stallion the whole last year. So. That tells me you didn't know."

Erica was amazed to hear herself saying very calmly, "I did know."

Nobody said anything. Elaine ordered a beer. Sue looked at Erica, and Jeannette said, "If you knew, why didn't you say anything?"

Erica reached across the table. There were things you could tell your friends and things you couldn't. She didn't know really just how honest she could be now. "I knew something was different. I didn't want to think what was different. I mean, Martin and I never had any problems; you know things went along very smoothly. We liked each other. But I sensed something, I suppose. I mean, I was getting very sad, very unhappy. I went to the doctor, he said there was nothing wrong, so"—Erica shrugged—"I figured there was nothing wrong."

"You're lucky he didn't tell you to whack off your tit," Elaine said, "or you would have done that, too."

Erica winced. "That's a little different."

"It all stems from the same source," Elaine said.

"What source?" Jeannette seemed concerned.

"The general attitude men have toward women, including men doctors, particularly men doctors," Elaine said. "They know what's best. If a woman has a serious attachment to her breast, she's emotional, which means she's not important. Doctors don't think emotions are important, because they're attached to women. Or breasts, either. You don't notice they recommend slicing off balls with total aplomb."

"That's a little different," Jeannette said.

Erica was upset. She was upset that she agreed with everything Elaine was saying. She thought so, too. But the venomous tone behind it surprised her, surprised her because she agreed with that, too.

"It's really no different," Elaine said. "Think about it."

"You're getting awfully radical," Sue said. Erica had not noticed that Sue had come in slightly drunk. Now it was noticeable. She couldn't have gotten drunk on two martinis.

"Yessirree," Sue was saying, "Erica's turning into a psychiatrist, and Elaine's becoming a libber. Must be what happens when you're not getting it." Sue smiled at them then in such a weird, hostile way, with such distance, that all of them including Elaine were suddenly taken aback.

"You're drinking a lot lately, Sue," Jeannette said quietly.

"That's because," Sue said, "I lost my job."

"What are you talking about?" Elaine said crossly. "You don't have a job."

" 'Course not. I have Roger," Sue said. "That's why I lost my job." None of them except Erica knew what she was talking about.

Elaine said, "I think we should put you in a taxicab."

"I think you should get laid," Sue said to Elaine, but loud enough for the entire room to hear. Several men at the bar began to laugh quietly, and began to stare at the table.

Erica stood up. "I think I'm going to leave."

Jeannette said, "Good idea. This isn't working out."

"Don't leave me here with the goods, kids," Elaine said, standing up. "All right, Sweetlips, either you get in a cab now, or we leave you here," she said to Sue.

"We can't leave her here," Jeannette whispered to Erica.

Erica turned to her. "Sure we can. She's not that

drunk. Good night, Sue," she said to Sue, and then to the other two, "I'll call you."

"Erica," Elaine ran after her, "what're you doing? We can't leave Sue here. Not with all those guys."

"What's the matter with you?" Erica suddenly wanted to get out. It was getting embarrassing. "They're not going to rape her."

"But they'll use her. They'll make an ass of her." Elaine looked so confused, Erica was momentarily touched.

They were nearly to the door when they turned around and saw that the man Erica had found so attractive was sitting down next to Sue. Sue was lapping it up and suddenly yelled out loud enough for everyone to hear, "No, I don't want to go *home*! I want to *fuck*! Sure I'm drunk, but I can still fuck when I'm drunk, but you can't, can you? Not when you're drunk. My husband *can't* when he's drunk, and he's always drunk! Hah!" The entire bar burst out laughing, and the man, smiling, got up and went back to the bar.

"I think she can handle herself," Erica said, dying for her, yet wanting to get away.

Elaine was right behind Erica. "She said 'fuck.' Sue never says 'fuck.' Did you hear that?"

Erica turned to Elaine. "You look absolutely shocked, which I think is hysterical. Do you think she doesn't know how to say it?"

"But she *doesn't* say it," Elaine said. "She's making an ass of herself. I'm surprised you don't care."

"Look, I'm not her mother," Erica said. "She's enjoying every minute of it."

"Should I call Roger?" Elaine asked.

"If I were you, I'd get in a cab. I'm sure Sue will call Roger."

"Why are you so sure?" Elaine was hurrying to catch up with Erica's stride. Erica just wanted to get out.

"Because she came in drunk. She must be mad at him—that's the only time she drinks—he must be out with somebody."

"He's always out with somebody."

"Well, maybe it's a close friend. How do I know? Elaine, I want to get out of there. I want to go home."

"Is that what you do when you get annoyed? You just pack up and leave?" Elaine stood in the doorway yelling after Erica.

"It's not the Girl Scouts, Elaine," she screamed. "It's not an overnight, and this is not the forest!"

"That's what you think," Elaine yelled back at her and turned back toward the bar.

Erica kept on walking, fast. Jeannette had quietly slipped out of the bar, she realized, without even saying good-bye. Suddenly she felt someone behind her, and turned around. It was the good-looking man at the bar.

"Hi," he said. "You walk fast. Are you a jogger?"

"No," Erica said, not slowing her pace.

"I tried to offer your friend a lift in a taxi, but she wasn't interested. Hey," he said, touching her arm, "I'd like to buy you a drink."

Erica stopped walking. She turned slowly and looked at him. He was very, very good-looking. Male-model type. Very rough-hewn.

"Do you pose for Marlboro ads?"

He smiled. "No, I don't pose, believe it or not. Now, can I buy you a drink?"

Erica shrugged. "I guess so," she said. She didn't know why in hell she said she guessed so when she really didn't want to. He was nice, he was gorgeous, she didn't really feel like going home. She ought to make the effort. Why not? So she went.

They made their way into a small neighborhood bar with a dance floor. After two drinks, he asked Erica to dance, and she did. He was a good dancer, beautiful to watch, graceful, sexy, practiced. Two more drinks and Erica was beginning to feel excited. But she wasn't going to go home with him. Not this time. One pickup was enough. She was surprised he didn't press her. When she said she had to go home, he hailed her a cab and got in, too. And he didn't even try to kiss her during the trip home.

When they got in, Patti was reading in the living room. Ken Platt, which was his name, as it turned out, said goodnight to her at the door, and Patti looked up for just a minute and said "Hi."

He said "Hi," nodded to her, and left. Erica came in and threw her coat down on the sofa. She noticed something strange in Patti's expression. A subdued quality.

"Don't you like him?" Erica asked.

"I don't know, but he sure is pretty," Patti said.

"You noticed that, too," Erica said.

"Yeah, he looks like one of *those guys from the Marlboro ads*," they both said together.

"I didn't know you had a date," Patti said.

"I didn't. He picked me up after one of our group meetings."

"Not bad for a pickup, Mom," Patti said. "You want a Coke?"

"Yes." Erica sat down, put her feet up, and looked at the book Patti was reading. *The Crisis of Adolescence.*

"Are you having a crisis, Patti?" she said, surprised.

"Yes," Patti said, her mouth beginning to quiver.

"What is it?" Erica was suddenly concerned.

"I'm, I'm, I—" Suddenly the tough, confident Patti crumbled and began to cry. "I miss Daddy, I miss Daddy, I want him to come home." She was sobbing now in Erica's lap. "I'm so unhappy, Mommy, I am." She was really in a state, Erica could see, and she did what she could to calm her, feeling suddenly horribly self-centered that she had not seen what it was, how deep the hurt was for Patti.

"Patti, maybe you can spend this weekend—I mean, you really haven't spent any time with him, and you'll feel better."

"I'm not going over to his house," she said, sitting up. Erica knew why. "I'm not. I'm not meeting this girl friend he's got."

"Who told you about that?"

"Phil."

"Phil. God, the local news agency. How does Phil know?"

"His mother told him. Everyone knows." Patti stood up. "It's the big joke that my father found his new girl friend in Bloomingdale's. Everyone thinks it's hysterical." She was sitting down again. "Mommy, I think I want to go away for a while."

"Where do you want to go?"

"I don't care, anywhere. I just want to go away."

"It's the middle of school."

"Please, Mommy." Erica was shocked at her daughter's face. The child was in agony. "I need to do something to get myself together. I'll go anywhere. Just a week."

"Patti, running away won't help. You've got to have this out with your father."

"Please." Patti began to cry again, and Erica couldn't take it, couldn't bear to see the normally imperturbable Patti in such a state.

"O.K., darling, maybe California. Perhaps your grandmother. I know she'd love to have you. Would you like to go there?"

Patti, still whimpering, nodded. "I want to go right away. Tomorrow."

"Patti, did you have a fight with Phil?" Erica asked, it suddenly occurring to her.

Patti nodded. "I have to go away, Mom. I'll feel better once I'm away. I'm going to bed." And tears still falling down her face, she kissed her mother goodnight and went into her room.

Erica sat for a while in the living room, simply staring into space. Life seemed to roll over her, these days. She felt she had lost direction, lost plans, lost confrontations. One day at a time had turned into a morass. She had to confront Martin. She had to. She picked up the phone and dialed.

Martin had said "only in emergencies," so she knew it was that girl's apartment. The girl answered.

"This is Erica Benton. I'd like to speak to Martin," Erica said.

"Oh, hi," the voice said. "I've heard so much about you. This is Marcia Brenner. I'll get him."

Boy, oh boy, Erica thought, her hand shaking, she wins the Welcome Wagon award of the year.

Martin's voice sounded strained. "What's the matter?"

"Sorry to disturb you," Erica said, "but I think we had better arrange to meet, and soon."

"What's the trouble?" Martin asked.

"Several things. Patti's very upset, for one thing. She wants to go to California to visit my mother."

"Well, O.K., I'll pay for it," Martin said. Erica winced. Every time she said anything these days, Martin said, I'll pay for it. "What else?"

"There are several other elses I'd rather not go into just now," Erica said. "We have to arrange to meet."

"O.K.," Martin said, not very helpfully.

"Well, when can you do it?"

"I don't have my calendar," Martin said.

"Well, how about Monday lunch?" Erica said.

"I might have a lunch date."

You *prick*, Erica thought, but she kept her temper.

"Well, after lunch," Erica said. "Look, Martin, I

don't want to do this any more than you do. But I think we'd better get some things straightened out. You must have *some* time on Monday."

"O.K. Monday lunch, I'll cancel whoever it is," Martin said. He didn't sound exactly anxious to see her. She hated talking to him, hated this entire exchange. He was probably sitting naked on that girl's bed.

"Twelve thirty," Erica said. "Where?"

"The Plaza. Is that O.K.?" Martin said.

"No."

"Oh," Martin said. Then he must have remembered. "Where would you want?"

"Four Seasons," Erica said. "The grillroom."

"O.K.," Martin said, "I'll make the reservation."

"Very generous," Erica said.

"Look, Erica, you're calling me at eleven at night on Friday to make a lunch date. I think I'm being quite generous. I told you this number was just for emergencies."

"Sorry I interrupted you," Erica said, "that it interrupted you and What's-her-face. Don't let me hold you any longer, Martin, but you shouldn't have answered the phone if you were in the middle of anything."

"Shut up, Erica," Martin said, and slammed down the receiver.

Good, she thought. She liked it all better when he was nasty. She wandered into the kitchen and stared out the window. She certainly was getting fresh. *And* hostile. That man she met tonight was nice. Something exciting about him. Something very rough, very tough about him. And she had a party to go to tomorrow night. That was good. And Patti. Which wasn't good. God, as bad as it was for her, it really was worse for Patti. A woman could love several husbands, but you only loved one father. Erica stayed a long time staring out the window, thinking of her own father. She remembered him only with affection, and a kind of longing she could never fully describe. He had died when she was seventeen, two years before she married Martin, and she missed him sharply still. When she allowed herself to think about it. Which wasn't often. Her mother had been wonderful. Was still. Her mother would be glad to have Patti. Would reassure her. Her mother had an openness, a warmth that Erica envied, that she would never have. And of course her mother would now know the truth. Erica blushed to think of it. It was ridiculous, but nonetheless she felt humiliated to confess to her mother that Martin had left *her*. She had told her mother that she'd left him, but now she'd have to tell her the truth. Why did it matter? Because she couldn't bear her mother to think she was unwanted—the beautiful, perfect, straight-A Erica? That that would disappoint her mother? Erica sighed. How absurd, how ridiculous we all were, she thought, staring out at the moonless night. Always that small sense of pride protected against the world, and our mothers. And the funny thing was, her mother would never judge her. Her mother would always take her side, think Martin the fool. Although her mother did like Martin, Erica knew that. Well, she sighed, and pushed herself away from the window. She had a party to go to tomorrow night. She had met a nice man. She had no reason to feel depressed. And yet. That phone call had done it. Martin was fucking someone else. It was one thing to be left. It was one thing for a marriage to dissolve. But it was quite another to be left for someone. That was the bitter pill. And that it had been going on, and she had acted as if she didn't know. She had and she hadn't. What was she supposed to have said? Anything would have been ridiculous. What was it? What had she done wrong? The question nagged at her as she tried to sleep. Yes, she did want Martin back. No, she hated Martin. It was all over. Burned out. Maybe this new man. She had steady fantasies about Ken Platt as she went to sleep—sweet, sexy fantasies, somewhat violent fantasies—he gave off the feeling of being a sexual powerhouse. Something in her was slightly afraid, something not.

She was surprised when he called her in the morning.

"Hi," he said.

"Hi." She knew who it was. "It's ten A.M. Are you an early riser?"

"You aren't, I guess," he laughed. "I just thought I might try a last-minute cancellation."

"What do you mean?"

"I was hoping you'd have one, for this evening, so I could see you."

"Oh," Erica said. "Well, I have a party to go to."

"I'd really like to see you. What time will you be through?"

"Too late," Erica said, thinking, then hesitating. "Well, you could come with me, I suppose. It's in Connecticut."

"That doesn't sound like an enthusiastic invitation."

"No," she said, embarrassed, "it's not that. It's that all my friends will be there, you know, old friends from when I was married, and I uh, well, I feel funny."

"I'd like to go. It's up to you. What time should I pick you up?" He'd made up her mind.

"About seven. It's rather formal. I hope you don't mind."

"I have a white jacket always on tap," he said.

"Good. I'll see you at seven." She hung up the phone feeling oddly triumphant. Well, she would show up with a gorgeous man, that was one point in her favor. Barbara and Sam Berger had invited her to this party to meet one, she felt sure, so she'd show up with one, that was all. Erica knew the Bergers meant well, but she had felt peculiar about going alone. She didn't know why. She hated focusing on it. Also, Martin was a good friend of the Bergers, and Erica knew that they had met

Miss What's-her-face, and stupid, childish as it was, she didn't want to show up empty-handed. Or empty. She began to laugh. What Tanya would make of that. The constant pursuit of the Phallic Hero. She sighed and got up. The phone rang just as she got to the kitchen.

"Hi, Mrs. Benton. This is Phil. Is Patti there?"

"I think she's still sleeping," Erica said, wanting to wring his neck. "And she told me you had a fight."

"Well, she had the fight. I mean, she's really taking this all pretty hard—you know, the whole thing."

"Yes, I know, Phil." This kid irritated her sometimes.

"Well, would you wake her up?"

"No, I won't. I'll tell her you called, though," Erica said, "when she does wake up."

"Who is that?" Patti was suddenly standing, sleepy-eyed, in the hall.

"It's Phil," Erica said. "I told him you were sleeping."

Patti reached for the phone. "I told you I don't want to talk to you," she said into it.

Erica smiled as she turned and reached for the coffee. Yes, fifteen was complicated, but thirty-six was worse. She would never be able to reach for the phone and tell Martin she didn't want to talk to him anymore. At thirty-six when you were married and you didn't want to talk, you reached for a lawyer. Erica plugged in the coffee and opened the morning paper. She heard Patti arguing vehemently in the hall.

Then she remembered Jeannette. She had told Jeannette she would drive up with her to the Bergers'. She had forgotten they were all going to be there. Jeannette and Elaine, and maybe Sue and Roger. They all knew the Bergers. Elaine's country house was only a mile away, and it was certainly going to be one of the "events" of the season. Erica had agreed to go only on the promise that Martin wouldn't be there. "I just can't handle that yet, Barbara," she heard herself saying, and

Barbara, easy, soothing, "I wouldn't dream of it, Erica, you know that." But she didn't know. It was hard on their friends. Trying to be on both sides at once. Erica had dared to ask, "Did you meet his girl friend?"

"Marcia?" Barbara said. "Yes."

"What's she like?"

"Erica, that's unfair. But she's very nice, very young, very naive."

"What does he see in her, Barbara? Tell me the truth."

"Erica, the girl is young—twenty-five or something. Martin's forty-five. Does that tell you anything?"

"I'm only thirty-six," Erica said.

"It's the idea. She's so young," Barbara said.

"I don't get it."

"Don't try to," Barbara had said, and then asked Erica to stay after the party for the weekend. Erica remembered now that she had said perhaps she would. Well, she couldn't very well. Not with a date. She called Barbara.

"Hi, it's Erica. Look, I'm bringing a date."

"Fine, there's plenty of room," Barbara said. "What's his name?"

"Look, I mean, we can't stay over. I mean, I hardly know him. I met him last night. His name is Ken Platt. And he's gorgeous."

"Well, if he's so gorgeous, you have to stay overnight. I mean, if you're shy, I'm not," Barbara said giggling. Barbara was the least likely candidate in the world for an affair, Erica thought. She thought that Barbara and Sam were two of the happiest married people she knew. Or maybe the only. Barbara was pretty, fat, and happy. Not superfat, but fat enough. On a perpetual diet, but always easygoing. Sam was a nervous wreck, but a sweet nervous wreck who always seemed relieved to get home to Barbara. They had a huge house, full of the requisite children, three or four, Erica thought, two large dogs, and a housekeeper who made the best apple pie in the world. A perfect life, Erica thought, and then she smiled ruefully to herself as she remembered that there wasn't any such thing.

10

As Ken drove the car up to the driveway of the Bergers' house, Erica could see Elaine, in bright red in the middle of the lawn, doing some outlandish dance. She seemed to be wearing harem pants, as she was attempting to stand on her hands and lift her silver sandals into the air. A small crowd had gathered around her attempts to do this, and just as the car came to a stop, someone held her feet for her and Elaine began to walk on her hands.

"Oh, my God, I hope she's not drunk," Erica said, smiling at Ken.

"Who is that?"

"My friend Elaine, the whirling dervish there in the red pants."

He looked over toward Elaine. "She seems too well balanced to be drunk. Wasn't she with you last night in the bar?"

"Yes, we have a group, they'll all be here. Including the one you tried to put in a cab."

"I doubt she'll remember me," he said. "Come on." He opened the door for Erica and she got out. She was wearing a light blue clingy Halston dress that looked like it had been poured over her. Ken had brought her fresh flowers for her hair, which she appreciated, and which added the final smashing touch.

"You look terrific," Patti had said.

"Yeah, you really do," Phil had said with a surprised note in his voice.

"Watch it, that's my mother," Patti had said, dragging him off, laughing. But Erica was pleased. She knew that as far as looks went, she and Ken made a smashing couple. Erica liked him. On the long drive up, she realized how attracted she was to him. He had a kind of intensity that was extraordinary. And he was beautiful. She couldn't get over the fact that he seemed absolutely to have no intention of making a pass. She realized she would not have minded. Something in his intensity excited her. And his stories. It didn't exactly register, but somehow she had taken in the fact that two of the stories he had told her had been about drinking in bars, which was evidently something he spent a lot of time at, and violent fistfights. He had never been directly involved, but he seemed to have a lot of friends who were fast with their hands. Erica liked it.

"Erica, darling, how good to see you." Barbara Berger's warm, perfumed body was enfolding Erica while Sam stood behind her, beaming and pumping Ken's hand.

"Hi, darling, so good to see you," Erica kissed Sam and Barbara and introduced Ken.

"You look gorgeous," Barbara said. "I must say trauma agrees with you."

"It's no longer a trauma, that's why," Erica said. "It's a pleasure."

Barbara had her hand and was pulling her toward the lawn, and as they rounded the corner of the house, Erica had a full view of a magnificent swimming pool, which had three levels of rocks jutting out on it, and swimmers, and a beautiful lawn full of lanterns, candles, music, and guests.

Erica heard herself being greeted by someone.

"Erica, baby." It was Don Hartwood, and behind him was his wife, Tina, who greeted Erica with mock enthusiasm and a slight kiss on the cheek. Erica introduced Ken and began to talk to Don, who was asking how she was and of course the inevitable "What happened?"

What happened and what happened and what happened. People desperately want to know WHAT HAPPENED. Erica was quick. "Look, Don, if I knew what happened, it wouldn't have happened, you know?"

She could see how interested he was, and smiled to herself. It had been happening for months now since Martin had left. Men looked at her differently. And so did some women. Don's wife, Tina, was hovering nearby like a piranha. God, do they all think I'm after their husbands? It's only been a few months, Tina, she wanted to say, and then quickly, seeing Tina's face, the jealousy written on it, felt ashamed and fell silent. She had felt that jealousy also, when Martin would start "talking up" a good-looking woman. Martin was the king of conversation. Women were wildly attracted to him. He was good-looking but certainly not gorgeous, but when he started talking, they lined up. Erica was quiet enough so that Ken took her hand and excused them and got them over to another corner of the yard.

"I sensed boredom," he said to her.

"Well, there was a wife problem."

"What kind?"

"They don't like it when their husbands talk to me. Some of them, anyway. Divorced and separated women have a five-minute exposure limit." She smiled and followed Ken toward the bar. None of them had ever found her that attractive married. It was funny. Ha ha. It wasn't funny. What disturbed Erica was that she really had to bite her tongue to keep from yelling at Tina. Her hostility amazed her. Maybe because the other women were there: them. The Group. The girls. Elaine and Jeannette and Sue. Something in the four of them had been changing lately; it had grown harder and more competitive. And something else. There was a kind of female machismo in the air among the four of them. The use of the word *fuck* was only symptomatic of what was quietly becoming, in Elaine's phrase, their new "waterfront style."

With the exception of Jeannette. Jeannette was the only one who didn't on occasion resort to truck driver language and observation. Maybe, Erica sighed, taking the drink from Ken, there was something to the business about "getting it steady." She had certainly been more of a lady when she'd been married. But had she been more female? Ken had his hand lightly on her arm now and steered her toward the pool.

"I want to be alone with you," he said in mock seriousness.

"You've certainly come to the right place."

"Hi, Erica." She heard Elaine's voice and turned around. Elaine was with a tall, very large man who walked like a lumberjack. "This is Jack Raines," Elaine said, her eyes glued to Ken Platt. "And you look awfully familiar," she said in a way that made Erica know she recognized him.

"We met in P.J.'s the other night," he said, smiling and shaking the lumberjack's hand. Erica was wondering where he came from. Elaine hadn't mentioned this one. Although Erica suspected that there were a lot of men in Elaine's life that didn't get mentioned. Occasionally she would make a wry remark that she was Queen of the One-Night Stand, but she didn't talk about it. Mostly she talked about not having a man. What Erica realized, in the midst of this lavish party, was that her friends were in some way embarrassing to her. That Elaine and Sue and Jeannette were there was somehow embarrassing, because of what they talked about.

She excused herself after a minute with Elaine and walked off toward the far end of the gardens. Ken was behind her in a minute. "You look much too thoughtful for a party. Want to be alone?" he asked her.

"Oh, I don't know. I was just thinking about my friends. I'm embarrassed to be seen here with them."

"With your friends?"

Clearly he didn't understand. "Yes. I mean, they're not embarrassing at all, but what we share; I mean, we meet each week—I told you about that—and what we share there I feel awkward about here. Also they bring out a bitchiness in me that's getting out of hand."

"I don't think you're bitchy," he said softly.

"Oh, you don't know," Erica said, rolling her eyes, "when I get going, I make Stanley Kowalski look like Elizabeth Barrett Browning."

He was laughing. "I'd like to see that conversion."

"Well, you will." She turned to him. "Come on, I'll introduce you to some people you will like, and then I have to do a tour by myself." He nodded and followed her. He was so agreeable Erica couldn't believe it. For more than this, she thought, you cannot ask. Erica left Ken in the hands of Barbara and went into the house to find Elaine. She knew she'd been rude to her and she was sorry. Elaine was sitting in the living room, alone, with her shoes off. "Hi," Erica said.

"Hi, Friendly. Gee, I'm glad I know you so well," Elaine said. "You're a real champ to meet at a party."

"I'm sorry. I came to tell you I was sorry."

"It's O.K. I get picked up in bars, too, you know, you don't have to act so damn embarrassed."

Erica smiled. "You've only begun the evening—do your feet hurt already?"

Elaine said, "Yes. They are killing me because I've been on them since five P.M. Gorgeous out there, and I have been making the rounds of three or four cocktail parties before we got here."

"Where'd you meet him?" Erica asked. "You never said anything."

"He came to fix the roof yesterday and stayed the weekend."

"I see." Erica couldn't hide her surprise.

"Well, look, things get scary and lonely up here in the country. If you can't make out with the pool men, you're left with the guy at the country store. In the winter it's not bad, you have the skiers. But in the summer, forget it."

Elaine was trying to be funny. Except it wasn't funny. It made Erica angry. "I see," she said. "Well, he certainly is *big*. Tell me, can he talk?"

"Oh, yeah," Elaine said. "He talks, he walks, does the whole thing."

"I think I'll go find Ken," Erica said, hearing someone moving in the next room. She had thought they were alone.

"Erica, is he nice?" Elaine asked.

"Yes."

"I mean really nice," Elaine said.

Oh, God, Erica thought. Oh God oh God oh God. I don't believe it. "He's nice," she said, and left the room. What was this desperation? This search for The One. The joke about Mr. Right had never left the planet, not for these women. Him. He. Is He. Did You. What's He Like. I need a man. The focus for the four of them, week in week out, was The Man. Your man. A man. This had always been true, but Erica was now understanding it in a new way. It was supposed to be a meeting about themselves as women. All it did was raise their consciousness about how desperate they were for men. Men at a weekly poker game might on occasion discuss women. And sex. They might discuss it every week. But surely sometime, part of the time, they talked about poker. Erica realized they never did. Oh, they talked about how they felt, sometimes, but then it was as if they were so embarrassed at the despair with which they discussed themselves that they immediately launched into the Man. The Perfect Man. The Perfect Relationship. Perfect Perfect Perfect. And their Erica, the Perfect Ideal, had gone and done this to them. Proved it wasn't true. There was no perfect. And less than perfect was no good. It certainly wasn't good in Sue's relationship with Roger. But none of them—Erica even had to admit this herself—would even accept the one that worked, which was Jeannette's. They wouldn't accept it because they didn't like it. Jeannette had not found Mr. Perfect. Jeannette, in their eyes, had found some agreeable jerk. It was true he was young, but that wasn't why they rejected the relationship. There was too much equality in it, Erica knew. Not enough fantasy. She knew this, and somehow in the midst of this evening she was knowing it in a way that had never been driven home before.

It was dark now, and the lighted torches circling the lawn lit up the profiles of trees against the sky in a magnificent display. The moon was out, and some people were still swimming. Erica felt like it herself. She hadn't gone very far when she ran into Don Hartwood, who was, of all things, being hung on by Sue. Sue was drunk again. Erica was shocked. She hadn't realized how far things had gone with Sue. The worst of it was she was literally draped across Don, who was obviously enjoying it all immensely. Erica wanted to get away, but she couldn't.

"And here's the beautiful Erica again," Don was saying. Sue was rubbing up and down his arm. Erica saw Sue's husband, Roger, not ten feet away, eyeing the entire spectacle, carefully.

"Isn't this the sexiest man you've ever ever seen?" Sue said, rubbing against him, taking his hand, looking into his eyes.

"Oh, yes," Erica said, feeling like an idiot.

"She gets prettier every year, this little Susie," Don was saying. He had a leer on his face.

"You're just saying that 'cause you know I love it," Sue was saying back to him. Now she had Don's hand on her chest, holding it smack across her rather full breasts. Sue always wore low-cut dresses, so Erica was not at all surprised to see them arrayed in full display. What surprised her was that Sue was all but taking the guy to bed with her and Roger was watching it. Erica thought Sue knew Roger was watching.

"Erica, Erica"—Don had his arm on her shoulder—"isn't it something to see your good friends like this? I mean, isn't it really terrific how the same people stay friends year after year? I mean, hell, Erica, I felt awful when I heard about you and Martin. But after all, marriages come and go, but friends stay the same. Isn't that the truth." Sue was nuzzling his neck as he said this, and he turned toward her, his hand stroking her backside.

"I think Sue's drunk," Erica said to Don.

Sue turned to Erica, a strange look, but one of total sobriety in her eyes. "No, I'm not, Erica. Tonight I'm not drunk. But I am hot, you're right about that," and she went back to nuzzling Don's neck.

Erica left them and went to look for Ken. Barbara came up to her. "That guy is a real honey. I think he went inside to watch TV or to look for you," she said.

"Oh, hi. O.K."

"Your friend Sue is really after Don Hartwood tonight," Barbara said.

"Yeah, and Roger's standing right there."

"Oh, well, nothing new about that. He's never less than ten feet away."

"Even when she's doing that?"

"Well, she's always doing that," Barbara said. "I guess that's the deal."

"What are you talking about?" Erica asked, feeling stunned.

"Oh, you know how she carries on at parties. I

mean, it's always been true, and Roger just watches. He doesn't interfere. He doesn't say anything, not until it's very late. Then there's always a scene. I guess she feels justified because he's always screwing around. I don't know."

"Oh," Erica said, so disturbed at this news about Sue she was speechless. "Always, Barbara? You mean Sue's been behaving like this for years? I thought it was Roger who was. . . ."

"Oh, that's only half of it," Barbara said. "She usually gets drunk. She isn't now, she's high as a kite, but she usually gets drunk. In fact, one year at the Steins' New Year's party, they found her in bed with Eliot Stein. Eliot had passed out, so I don't even think anything went on, but Roger dragged her out, naked as could be, screaming the whole time, into the living room, dragged her through the living room, buck-naked, into the snow and into the car."

Erica was shocked. She was visibly shocked. So much for the honesty of their little group. She had never heard this story. "What happened?" Her voice sounded small.

"I don't know. She got a cold, that's all I ever heard about it. I think they hate each other. I don't know why she stays."

"She can't leave," Erica said.

"I know," Barbara said. "But it's really about the worst marriage I've ever seen. I don't know if he even ever sleeps with her."

"Oh, yes," Erica said, no longer feeling she was betraying a confidence. "Every time he breaks up with a girl friend—about once every six months—he comes home to her. They ball for a week, and it's great. Then he finds a new girl." Erica's voice was bitter.

"It's so depressing," Barbara said.

"Yeah. I think I'll go find Ken."

"He looks like a good one to find."

"Look, Barbara, if I found God tomorrow morning, I couldn't be seriously interested. You know, things take time."

"I forget it hasn't been that long. Sorry, Erica."

Barbara hadn't meant anything by it, but Erica was getting sick of this business—find, find, find. Jesus Christ, women made you think that finding a man was discovering a pot of gold.

11

Erica knew that the party had put her in a perfectly dreadful mood. Somehow, seeing Elaine and Sue in this kind of situation had depressed her terribly. Elaine she really was not surprised about. She had been surprised only at the accepted casualness with which Elaine had referred to her date. The idea of a permanent life of nothing but casual sex had upset Erica; she really had never believed Elaine had led a life where men seemed to drop in and out as casually as if she were a motel. It depressed her, it angered her, and it revolted her, all more or less at the same time. Why them? she thought, why should they depress me so much, they're not *me*, I'm me; but even as she thought it, she knew why: it was too much failure. It was too much. All the more she understood why she, Erica of the perfect marriage, had been so very important to them. Sue and Elaine had at that moment the most unperfect lives imaginable to Erica—she didn't want to be near them. But she had to admit that Elaine, at least, had some shred of honesty about her. But Sue—Sue, Erica felt, had lied to her completely. And seeing Sue literally slobbering all over Don Hartwood like a horny out-of-town salesman, half-drunk and clearly desperate, had revealed a side of Sue Erica couldn't face. She couldn't face the fact that here was a woman who, on the superficial evidence, did not have a bad life. She was married, she had two grown children—with whom she had, admittedly, lousy relationships, but they were both in college, so the relationship did not look too lousy except at Christmas when they came home, because in the summer they never did—and a husband with whom she was so busy being angry and reconciling that everyone had assumed there was *some* kind of relationship. Erica saw it all suddenly differently. There was not a relationship between Sue and Roger; there was a pattern, a situation of breaking up and reconciling, that *was* the relationship. And in between the reconciliations, this woman went about seducing neighbors, friends, whatever man she could lure to her bed, making a public scandal of her rage and receiving only pity for it. What really was reaching Erica, she knew, was that she had always liked Sue, respected her because she felt sorry for her, because Roger was the *bad* one; and especially after her conversation yesterday with Sue, she had felt particularly sad about the fact that Sue obviously felt she had sacrificed a great deal in marrying Roger. She had even called Elaine to ask, "What was the big deal? What did she give up?"

Elaine said, "Oh, hell, I don't know. She used to design greeting cards or something. I mean, she is a terrific designer—just look at their house—but I don't know why she just gave it up. I mean, you know Roger never said anything about she had to. I mean, there was enough money there; it wasn't as if she had to stay home and take care of the children; you know she could have kept her own business. She just kept saying Roger had to be first all the time, and first and first and first and first suddenly one day became only. Only Roger and no work. I don't know what happened. You've heard her talk about it. She's got some idea he drained it all out of her—you know, all that stuff about what women sacrifice in marriage. God, Erica, you've heard it enough from her. Why are you asking me?"

"Because I still don't know what she meant. I mean, I do and I don't."

"Look, Erica," Elaine had said in that savage way she had, "you know what she said. She's a heavy case, but you know what she's talking about. I don't like to talk about it, either."

"Martin never drained anything out of me," Erica was saying, hearing the defensiveness in her voice.

"I noticed what an impressive career you have."

"Careers, ca-shmeers, why is a hot job in a business office suddenly such a big thing? Show me so many men with careers!" she had screamed at Elaine over the phone.

"Erica"—Elaine's voice sounded tired—"you're my friend and I'd like to keep you my friend and this conversation makes me very tired. You know? So let's drop it," and she hung up.

That conversation had stayed in the back of Erica's mind, playing on her in what she thought was not a totally honest way. I mean, she used to think, it was true Martin never made me give up my work, but it did become less important. It did. She realized in some peculiar way that Martin had become her work. She had devoted herself to him. And yet she had held back so much. God, there it was again, the yes and the no; she had certainly put her work out of her life, except for those few weeks in the summer, and she had, in a large sense, devoted herself to Martin. Devoted. Somewhere the word nagged at her. Yes, she had made Martin a project in a sense, and yet it was true, she knew, too, that she had devoted herself to him, and not given herself. She had known it that first night she went to bed with Charlie, when she *had* given herself, and it had surprised her, moved her, exhilarated her, and, in the most profound sense, shocked her. She hadn't known what she was holding back until it came out. She had never thought she was sexually inhibited, but something certainly had been held back, something that belonged to Erica, made her herself, her own, that something she had never given to Martin, and she knew it. Did he?

"Hi." Ken Platt was at her arm again, his voice soft in the dark, the pressure on her arm firm and warm. They were on the edge of the party, which was breaking up now. The moon was very low in the sky, the sounds of people saying goodnight, car doors slamming—it was the moment at parties that Erica usually liked. Tonight it made her sad. And this man felt like a stranger to her, a nice friendly handsome attractive stranger, but very far, very distant, perhaps because she herself felt so lost in who she was and what she wanted. Confusion. She had never really known the meaning of the word. She just knew that in the midst of the party she had come to something, some understanding of herself in relationship to men, to marriage, to her friends, that she had not anticipated. And she didn't like it.

"I think we should go, don't you?" he said to her.

To her surprise, Erica found herself saying, "It's later than I thought, too late to drive. If it's all the same to you, we can stay over until the morning."

A brief look crossed his eyes, which she couldn't quite read. Then he said, "Whatever you want."

She grabbed his hand and said, "Barbara has a thousand rooms here. I know she wouldn't mind." The fact was she was too depressed to get into a car and talk. She needed something else—she didn't know what—but she didn't want to drive back. Not then, not with him.

Barbara, of course, as Erica knew, was only too happy to make the arrangements, despite the fact that she was surprised when Erica insisted they have separate rooms.

"All right, anything for appearances' sake," Barbara

said, "but you're right across the hall, and you're both in double beds."

"If I didn't know better," Erica said, "I would have to say that you are deliberately trying to arrange something, something with definite sexual implications."

"Let me tell you something," Barbara said, "vicarious experience can be a real thrill," and then she laughed and Erica didn't quite know how to take it. She shrugged and went inside.

Ken said goodnight to her in the hall, stroking her hair, and then leaned over and kissed her gently—*too* gently. Erica was somewhat surprised, in fact very surprised. She pulled his head back toward her, wanting at least a kiss that was a kiss, and when she did that, he responded, and when he did, she was certain he was coming into her room later. After she had undressed for bed, she lay awake with only one light burning, thinking about Patti, who was staying at Phil's for the night, wondering if she was sleeping with him, unable to bear the idea, wondering if she should have gone home, deciding no, wondering how long it would take him to come into her room.

Eventually Erica fell asleep, somewhat angry, somewhat disappointed, somehow fearful that suddenly she was very very alone. She didn't know why, but she woke up about five o'clock that morning feeling very warm. She went to the window and opened it and stood there for several minutes. She knew what she was doing, making up her mind. She had to admit there was something of a turn-on in walking out of her room, stark naked, across the small hall, and into his at five o'clock in the morning. He was sleeping on his back, one arm thrown across his head, and she thought he really was vulnerable-looking, all that stuff about sleep and vulnerability was hopelessly true. She stood for a moment in the door, feeling suddenly silly. What if she couldn't wake him up? She didn't want to be caught standing up naked in his room. She went back into her room, got on a robe, and then went back and sat on his bed. He woke up quickly.

"Hi," he said, pulling her to him, and without another word, opened the covers and pulled her in. He kissed her and stroked her, but, she thought, without passion. Finally, kissing the top of her head, he held her and said, "You know, we don't have to make love. We can just lie here," and she felt so peculiar hearing it she hardly knew what to make of it. She, after all, had come to him. Why did he have to explain she didn't have to feel compelled.

She kissed him on the mouth and rolled on top of him. "I know we don't have to," she said, now determined to go through with it, and he responded, holding her, kissing her, and somehow the lovemaking became for Erica an exercise in estrangement such as she had never known. He was polite, she thought, even practiced, sensitive, and capable as a lover, but the intensity which had attracted her to him was missing. There was so little that was forceful, she felt even his drive to climax was almost reluctant. She had never imagined a man could give her so little. Of course, afterward she thought of Charlie. But what about Charlie? Charlie wasn't the answer in his intensity any more than this man was the answer in his tenderness for her. He had held her and cuddled her and made Erica feel generally like a baby, or a well-loved cat. It was not a mood or a temper she could like. He was a nice man. And that was about it.

When Erica woke up the next morning, sheer terror overtook her. Groping, she found her way to the bathroom and stared at the drawn, blank look on her face. The weekend surrounded either by people she knew who disappointed her or by those who didn't know her, the weekend surrounded by defining herself, had taken its toll. She had been tempted last night to get very drunk, with dramatic thoughts of flinging herself in the swimming pool, and of course drowning, champagne glass in hand—there would be lots of pictures. The *Daily News* would give her a spread: WOMAN IN $400 HALSTON DROWNS SELF IN POOL. It would certainly serve Martin right. She had been defining herself in terms of Martin so much she recognized now that she was even prepared to die in terms of Martin. God. Was this love? No, she knew it wasn't, somehow. It had nothing to do with love and everything to do with insecurity, but then so did Charlie, and in a funny way she was so fond of him. And he excited her, and yet she had to know she could walk out anytime, and come back anytime. Erica knew it would have to end. There had to be a time limit on how long you could get away with doing this—but on the other hand, the sheer, exhilarating power of it. And then earlier, the total absence of feeling—she felt like shit. She realized she wanted to think Charlie could cure that. But she knew somehow he couldn't. That was over, too.

The drive back was pleasant enough. He was affectionate, caring, and Erica thought had no idea how she really felt. It was the oddest thing. Absolutely as if it hadn't happened. For some peculiar reason, it had made her realize even more strongly what strange territory she had been inhabiting the last few months. She didn't belong to Martin, she couldn't belong to Charlie, and this man in his isolation had made her realize she didn't want to be in a suspended state of *not* giving herself to anyone. She knew now, after the party, that for a lot of reasons she had to see Martin one more time. She had to get things straight.

12

"WHAT DO YOU MEAN, you're seeing Martin for lunch tomorrow?" Elaine said, almost speechless. "Are you dating or something? You just saw him two weeks ago."

"I know, but I couldn't talk to him. We have something to discuss."

"I never heard of so much discussion. What all are you discussing?"

"Our sex life."

"Your sex life?" Elaine, for once, was dumb.

"Yeah, his with her, mine with whoever, sometimes with myself."

"Erica, you sound tough, but you melt like jelly."

"Coming from Humphrey Bogart I could listen to that. From you it's awful."

"You'll never be Katharine Hepburn."

"I'll never wait till I'm forty-five to get screwed in a steamer going downstream, either."

There was a pause. "It's awful, isn't it?"

"What?"

"Seeing Martin."

"Ycah." Erica didn't know what to say. Then she changed the subject. "How's the lumberjack?"

"He dropped me off, you know, and he really dropped me. I guess I didn't tell you."

"No, what?"

"Well, when he dropped me off, he said"—Elaine's

voice seemed to catch—"he said he wasn't coming in, which, you know, surprised me because to tell you the truth he's somethin' else in the sack." That was Elaine. "I mean, it was really good."

Erica thought she sounded upset about it. "Well, what *happened*, Elaine?"

"Christ, Erica, we're getting awful. I felt like two cents."

"Well, what did he say?"

"He quoted me."

"What was it?"

"He said, 'I'm not coming in,' and I said, 'Why not?' And he said, 'Because I walk, I talk, I do the whole thing.' Then he slammed the door and drove off."

Erica blushed. She remembered now, there was someone in the house when she was talking to Elaine.

"So what did you do?"

Elaine sighed, "Nothing. I couldn't apologize and say I didn't mean it, because I did mean it. And he knew it. Every once in a while I discover I have really crummy values."

Erica said nothing, then, "I'll call you in a few days," and she hung up. The conversation depressed her. Just one more piece in the mounting evidence that if anyone was going to save Erica, it was going to have to be Erica.

13

THE LUNCH WITH MARTIN was possibly one of the most horrible moments in Erica's life. She had never felt such unremitting hatred for anyone as she did for this man sitting across the table from her, the salad drooling out of his mouth, trying to fence her questions, embarrassed, shameful, some heap of a man trying to make sense for her, trying not to tell her the truth.

"This is the last time, Martin. I'm asking you *what happened.*" Her voice sounded like she was hissing. She hated sounding this way.

"I don't know what you mean," Martin said. This was the third time he had answered the question that way.

"I mean what the hell was going on? You were fucking me, Martin my love, while you were screwing her. In fact, if I have to say it, I have to tell you you were screwing me better than ever, the more you were screwing her. Oh, yes"—Erica could hear her voice building—"you were definitely screwing me better. Oh boy, oh boy, were you ever, because I know when you met her and I have a very good memory. Now tell me, Martin, what was it *I* didn't have? Now, before you answer"—she was enjoying the glazed look that had come over his face—"don't tell me I wasn't good in bed. I know my ratings are very high with any number of men. In fact some guy told me if I ever wanted to turn professional . . ."

Martin's hand shot out and slammed across her face, hitting her with a blow that stunned her momentarily and knocked her into the side of her chair. His voice was trembling, and he was screaming, "Shut up, shut up, shut up!" Martin had never talked like that in his life. He stood up now, shaking with rage, while Erica tried to recover, keeping back the tears.

"Well, Martin, but we liked each other, we fucked each other, we even had fights to prove how happy we were—and you, you fall in love with some nit in Bloomingdale's. I'd just LIKE TO KNOW WHY!" Erica was screaming now as Martin retreated out of the restaurant. She saw him disappearing down the stairs. "I'D LIKE TO KNOW WHY," she screamed, and then before she knew what had hit her, she raced down the stairs after him, reaching for his jacket. "Don't walk out on me until you answer this—do you hear me?"

Her face was wild, the scene was insane, she was insane. Martin's face was in a million pieces, and his voice, very far away, was very calm, very still. "What happened, Erica, which you will never understand, was she made me feel like king of the world. Do you know what that is? Somebody who thinks *you're* terrific, everything *you* do is important, who thinks you're simply wonderful? Do you know WHAT THAT IS?" Martin was screaming now, "NO, you don't know because you never thought that. You took everything for granted because you didn't need anything. You absolutely never *needed* anything I could give you. Nothing personal, absolutely nothing."

"You're full of shit," Erica said, wondering why he was talking in this way. Martin never talked like this. What was this—giving him something?

"Do you mean," she was shouting, her voice surprising her, "that I didn't lick your boots, that I was not *adoring*? I could have gotten you a cocker spaniel if I'd known your need was so desperate. I could have. . . ."

But Martin had walked away, left her standing there in the middle of the stairs, the waiter approaching anxiously, "Madam, the bill?" The nerve of him, asking her that when her husband was walking away in the middle of the stairs. The final humiliation was she had left her purse on the chair. She had to go upstairs, face the room of diners looking at her. She thought they were all staring at her, and she couldn't.

"Charge it," she said, leaving her purse and everything on the chair. She couldn't go back, and she raced down the stairs past the hatcheck girl, out the door after Martin. She was a maniac—she knew it as she reached for his arm and screamed, "Why didn't you go sooner? Why a whole goddamned year, Martin?!"

He shoved her arm away from him and turned to her, trembling. "Because it was good, O.K. Erica, hear this one and hear it right. The more I had her, the more I wanted you. The guiltier I got, the more it turned me on. She made me hot for you. She did it, not you. It had nothing to do with you. I was getting off on it, and I LIKED IT. Do you understand that?"

Martin turned on his heel and left her standing stunned in the street. Erica stared at his retreating back, and all she could think was, Over. Over. Over. Never had anything been more over than this.

She knew she was calling Elaine because she needed consolation. Life was perverse. She was also calling Elaine because she knew she wouldn't get it.

"You saw him for lunch?" Elaine screamed over the phone. "I thought you only met in lawyers' offices. What happened?"

"He told me she got him hot for me, that's what happened."

"Oh, God."

14

DURING THE NEXT FEW WEEKS Erica threw herself into her work at the gallery with a sense of exhaustion, frustration, and rage. The relief she felt was incredible. She felt the work was saving her from her sense of despair, from her friends and her mounting sense of uncertainty. She left right after Patti in the morning, and didn't get home until after eight o'clock, often going home finally only because of Patti. Herb appreciated it. At the end of the third week, Herb told Erica he was so impressed with her he was going to let her hang Saul Kaplan's show.

"By myself?" Erica was amazed.

"With him, of course, but he's easy. You know Saul always asks me to hang his shows with him. There's not another artist that lets me near their stuff."

"Well, Herb, maybe you should still." Erica felt strangely out of place.

"No, no, you can do it. Besides"—Herb smiled at her—"he asked for you to do it."

"He did? How would he know I'd be any good?"

"Well"—Herb gave her a fatherly smile—"I told him you did Larry's show."

She smiled. "With a lot of help from my boss."

"Yes," Herb said, "but still you did do a lot of it. Saul trusts you, that's the important thing. So do I. So go to it."

Erica felt absolutely silly being so pleased. But she felt like skipping all the way home.

"So why do you feel so silly?" Tanya asked.

"I don't know," Erica said. "I never thought I was really that good at anything that I could really try a show; you know, to me that's just amazing."

"Why are you so amazed?"

"I guess because I didn't really think I could do it. Simple but stupid, right?"

"There's more to it than that," Tanya said.

"I know." Erica looked at her feet. She was ashamed to admit how little she thought of herself, even to Tanya, much less to herself.

Erica had known Saul Kaplan well enough to speak casually to him, but of all the artists at the gallery he was the most private, the most self-contained, so she was very surprised when he came in the first day she was working on his show to tell her how pleased he was she'd be doing it. He wasn't effusive, but Erica was genuinely happy he seemed so pleased. She called Elaine that night to tell her.

"Well, I'm glad for you," Elaine said. "You're really coming up in the world. However, now I have to tell you something fabulous."

"Well, I know that doesn't mean a job," Erica said, almost bitterly.

"You guessed it. A man. And man, what a man. He's terrific, and I even think he likes me."

"Is he for sale, rent, or hire?" Erica said.

"Nothing. He's mine."

"Where'd you meet him?" Erica was surprised at the sound of her voice. She was sick and tired of all of this. All of it. The damn man game.

"I met him at a party, and to be perfectly honest, I

didn't think we had a thing going until we went to bed."

"Then why *did* you go to bed?" Erica asked.

"He convinced me," Elaine said, giggling. "And am I glad. He has an enormous cock."

"You always were the violent sort."

"Don't tell me that doesn't turn you on."

"All right, I won't." But it did. It always did. Elaine throwing out these little innuendos, these sweet seductions about the men she slept with. A cock like a battering ram. Christ. Erica wondered if she could sleep tonight. "I'm hanging up," Erica said.

"Why?"

"I'm waiting for a call."

"Anyone I know?"

"I hope not," Erica said. "The last thing I need is a hostile man." She hung up.

She was furious at Elaine. Once again. She was jealous. She imagined Elaine's weekend. Who said women didn't think of men as sex objects?

Erica was surprised that Saul asked her to join him for dinner the next night. She hesitated, said she was busy, was in the middle of an excuse, and then was embarrassed.

"Actually, Saul, I have a daughter at home I haven't seen much of. I have to get home very early."

"Well, make it very early, then," he said. And he meant it.

They had "dinner" at six, and he toyed with a salad. Erica smiled. "Herb says you work all night and sleep all day. He couldn't believe you were eating dinner at six."

He looked at her skeptically. "Herb's right. I don't lie so good." He leaned over the table in mock earnest. "Erica," he said, touching her hand, "can I tell you the truth?"

She nodded.

"I can't stand the idea of salad for breakfast."

"Is that *right*?" she asked, laughing.

He nodded and called over the waiter and began an elaborate negotiation for two fried eggs. After that, they walked through SoHo, Erica finding herself very talkative, very at ease. She liked him, and she knew she was attracted to him. But somewhere she felt everything was happening too fast. She really wanted to be away from a man she cared about for a while. Just by herself, she thought. When he kissed her good-bye, she knew there was something happening, and knew, too, that she would go to bed with him someday.

Two days later, Erica agreed to meet Saul at his loft to select one of his smaller canvases for the show. She knew when she walked in the door and saw his tall figure bent over the canvas in an intense concentration, saw his shirtsleeves rolled up and the musical quality of that concentration, she knew she would stay.

At six that evening she rolled over drowsily and said to him, "That was a very special afternoon, but now I have to get home to Patti."

His hand reached over her. "Oh, no, you don't go anywhere. Call her and tell her to meet us."

Erica felt herself stiffen. "No, absolutely not."

"Would it embarrass you?"

"It wouldn't make me feel good."

"She doesn't have to know I'm your lover," Saul said.

Erica was up now and getting dressed. "You're not my lover," she said; her voice sounded hard.

"You know what I mean."

"I'm not very good at hiding my feelings."

"What are your feelings?"

Erica felt he was pushing her. "I just slept with a man I barely know. Casual sex is not my bag. I didn't feel like fighting it, that's all."

"Look, I don't go to bed with every woman that walks in here."

"I know, but I—I went to bed with you partly because I just felt like going to bed with somebody I didn't have a lot of feeling about, and somebody that wouldn't have a lot of feelings about me. You're safe," she smiled sadly. "You hardly know me." She finished putting on her blouse and then, turning to him, said, "I just wanted to have something that wasn't complicated."

He stared at her. "How does it feel?"

She shrugged. "Sort of empty."

He laughed. "At least you're honest."

"Oh"—she was concerned she might have hurt him —"the sex was very good."

"You have a bizarre way of handing out compliments."

"It's the best I can do," Erica said, moving toward the door.

"I'd like to see you again," he said.

"I have to go."

"Answer me." His voice was tougher than she'd expected.

"I don't know." She hesitated at the door.

"Why did you flirt with me at the gallery if you were so disinterested?"

"It was mutual."

He sighed.

"Do you want to know how I really feel?" Erica said. "As soon as the sex was over, I wanted to bolt out of here. It's not your fault, Saul, but that's the way I feel about it."

"That's pretty hostile."

"I don't feel hostile, Saul. I like you."

He looked at her with a faint show of irritation. "Why don't you go home?" he said. "I'm developing a very large headache."

"My husband used to get headaches when I didn't want to have sex."

He smiled. "That poor son of a bitch must have had migraines."

She laughed and turned toward the door. "I'll see you later," she said.

The next day she told Tanya Saul had called and she had told him she wouldn't see him for a while. He sounded angry, but she didn't feel guilty. She was so caught up in her work, she thought it made it easier. She simply did not want to get involved, not now. The next day, she told Herb she would work only that day on Saul's show. After that, he'd have to do it himself.

"Why not?"

"Personal reason," Erica said. Herb nodded and, to her surprise, gave her absolutely no argument.

"O.K.," he said, "just help me hang these today."

She was in the middle of hanging one of the small canvases when Erica heard a tapping at the window. She turned to see a young woman with long blond hair waving through the window at her.

"We're closed," Erica yelled, but the woman kept tapping. Finally Erica went to the door and opened it. "Look, we're closed today. I'm sorry," she said.

The woman stared at Erica. "I'm Marcia Brenner," she said.

"I don't think I—" Then it came to her. "Oh."

"I wanted to talk to you." Erica couldn't believe it was happening.

"I can't," she said, closing the door.

"I have to. It's important. I could meet you later."

"Just a minute."

Erica went back to the gallery. "I have to take a break for a few minutes, Herb."

Herb nodded; she grabbed her jacket and went out the door. Now what? she wondered. She's probably going to ask me to go easy on his money at the lawyer's.

"Well," Erica said, standing on the sidewalk, "what do you want?"

"I never went out with a married man in my life. This thing with Martin just happened."

"He told me," Erica said. Funny, Erica always thought she would want to kill her when she saw her. She didn't want to kill her. She just wished she would disappear.

"Martin's terribly guilty about it," she said.

"That's his problem."

"Look—" she started again.

"You look," Erica said. "Martin wants to be forgiven and he sends *you*?"

"He doesn't know I'm here. That would make him guiltier."

"I can't help you. I don't want to help you."

"You'd feel better, too. It would make everything better."

"How the hell do you know how I feel?"

"I'm a woman."

"You're a kid. You don't know anything."

"I'm old enough, Erica. Can I call you that?"

Erica sighed and looked at the sidewalk. This was nuts. "This is crazy," she said.

"I saw this French movie," Marcia went on. She seemed intent on it, so Erica decided to hear her out. "And a man got on an airplane and he saw the stewardess take her high-heeled shoes off and put on her slippers. He fell in love with her and his wife found out and in the end she came into a restaurant and shot him."

"I saw it."

"I thought it was a fantasy when I saw it."

"I'm not going to shoot Martin."

"He told me about this awful lunch. You said terrible things to each other."

"That's an understatement," Erica said.

"Let him come over and see you."

"Absolutely not."

"Please."

"Look, no. We had our lunch, that's it. Now I'm talking to a lawyer. It stinks. It's rotten, the whole thing. Why do you care? You ought to be relieved we're not talking to each other."

"I guess I want him to stop talking about you. When we were . . . seeing each other before, we just talked about 'The Problem.' Now that there is no problem, we've got a new problem."

Erica couldn't help laughing. "Look, whatever you've got, you've got. But I'm out of it now. That's all."

"Did he tell you about California?"

"What?"

"He might move to California. He's worried he won't be able to see Patti."

"Any time he sends a ticket he can see her. Look, I'm sorry, but there's nothing I can do."

Erica turned and went back into the gallery, leaving the girl standing on the sidewalk. She was sweet, and somehow helpless. That must be what turned Martin on. As she started inside, the girl rushed toward her.

"I like you. I wish we could be friends."

"That's another movie," Erica said, and closed the door.

Erica hadn't heard from Saul for three days when he called her and told her he wanted to see her.

"I don't know," she said.

"Look, Erica, be honest with me."

"I"—she hesitated—"Saul, I'll call you." And she hung up. He's going to hate me, she thought, and rightly so. I'm crazy. I like him. I really like him, and I can't stand the idea that I do.

* * *

"Look, Tanya," she found herself saying, "I just don't think I'm ready for a commitment thing."

"You only went to bed with him once. Why do you feel it would be a commitment thing?"

"Because"—Erica hesitated—"with him it would."

"Do you mean he's possessive?"

"No, he isn't. I'd feel like it was a commitment."

"Are you saying you feel very strongly about him?"

"No, of course not!" Erica said, her cheeks burning.

"You seem embarrassed," Tanya said quietly.

"Oh, hell, I'm very attracted to him. You know, I feel like he's a real person. I mean, if I got into a thing with him, I'd really be in. And I don't want that right now. I want to work."

"You feel you cannot do both—is that it?" Tanya asked.

"That's how I feel," Erica said. "I mean, just last weekend I started a painting—me, a real painting—not just fooling around. I mean, whether it's good or not isn't the real issue. I just felt so good doing it. I felt like myself. So possessed, so there, such divine concentration. I need that for a while."

"You said you were lonely."

"I am, but I'm afraid, too. More afraid of being involved than of being alone."

"You sound like you know what you want, about what sacrifices you are willing to make."

"I sound like it, but I'm still not *sure.*"

"You must be very attracted to him."

"Yes," Erica said.

15

ERICA FINALLY AGREED to go back to "the group," after three weeks of not showing up, mostly because Elaine pressured her into it. She asked them to meet her at the Spring Street bar, and she went right from the gallery, paint-spattered jeans and all.

"My God," Elaine said, "I don't know whether you are SoHo chic or this is the high art of rebellion. Let us admire your paint splotches. Come in."

"Hi, Erica, you look great," Sue said evenly. "I hear it's really final with Martin."

"You're the only one who never thought it wasn't. I told my lawyer to file for divorce. He says Martin doesn't want one."

"How's Patti doing?" Jeannette asked.

"O.K., I guess. She wants to go to California, but I'm undecided about pulling her out during the school year."

Erica sat down easily and ordered a beer. In a way she was glad she had come. They had stopped looking like vampires to her.

"Why haven't you shown up for three weeks?" Sue asked suddenly.

"Oh, I've been busy. You know, started painting again."

"Really? Tell us why," Elaine said pointedly, and Erica blushed.

"Well, you know, I guess. I mean, Elaine knows. At that party, I felt you all were so desperate, for men, for attention, I just couldn't stand seeing it." She turned to Sue. "Especially you."

"Warm, kind, understanding Erica," Sue said sarcastically. "Catching me in my slovenly drunk phase, hated me on sight." Erica's cheeks burned again. "You must hate yourself, then," she said quietly.

"Honestly, Sue, I don't know why you stay." Erica's voice was high-pitched. "I mean, what is in that sick thing with Roger and you?"

Sue sighed. Elaine and Jeannette were very quiet. "Look, to some extent it's none of your business, but hard as it may be for your rational, your ruthlessly rational little heart to know, there is something in it for me. What's in it for me is Roger, and a profound conviction that when I don't hate him I love him. There are not many people I can love, and that's important."

"But for *you*—what do *you* get out of it?" Erica said. "He doesn't act very loving toward you."

"He does," Sue said defensively, "sometimes. But you're right. What's in it for me is that sometimes I really feel I love him, and it's a foreign emotion to me in every other phase of my life, so I hang onto it." The sharp, bare impact of her words struck them with a quiet force that left them all temporarily speechless.

"Well," Elaine said, "the lady is her own crystal ball," and then was sorry she'd said it.

Sue glared at her. "Thanks for the support, friends," she said sharply, and pushed back her chair. "I've learned to dislike you all intensely, most particularly for your inability to tolerate anything other than your own grand and glorious life plans. Well, look at you. All of you. I'm the only one with a husband, and you think I've got the problem. Well, this is real life, ladies, and crystal ball or no crystal ball, if I'm not holding all the aces, at least I'm holding one. You're not holding anything, not even you," she said viciously to Jeannette. "Some kid who can't even earn a decent living."

She turned to Erica, "The beautiful bright perfect Erica had a husband that walked. Well, my marriage might be lousy, but my husband will never walk." She stalked out.

"Well," Elaine said, "I think I shouldn't have made the crystal-ball remark."

"I think," Erica said, "we haven't been very good friends. I mean, we do act superior to her."

"It's terrible. She thinks she's superior because she's in this nightmare of a marriage," Jeannette said. "And she thinks she's holding an ace."

"But all we ever do tell her, lately, is that she's screwed up," Erica said.

"Well, she is," Elaine said.

"I know. But you know, you have to have more going on in a relationship than that."

"Yeah, well, actually I think this group has deteriorated somewhat," Jeannette said.

"How?" Elaine asked.

"Well, I don't know. We don't go far enough sometimes, and sometimes we go too far. I mean, in the beginning I felt we were all in it together, and then, I don't know, at some point I just felt like we were all drifting."

"When Martin walked," Erica said quietly. The others didn't say anything.

"Why should that affect *us* so much?" Elaine asked, genuinely puzzled.

"I don't know," Erica said, "but it did."

"Tell me about the girl friend's visit," Elaine said, starting to laugh. "I mean, it's just too good to be true."

So Erica told them about Marcia, and Patti, and something about herself. But she didn't even mention Saul. And she knew then that it meant she had decided to see him.

16

ALTHOUGH ERICA HAD MADE up her mind she would see Saul, she didn't call him all week. She suspected she would see him Saturday night at Jean's loft; she was just hoping he wouldn't have a date, but she couldn't bring herself to call him. She just couldn't. In a mad moment, a last attempt to make up to Sue and hold the group together, Erica had invited Elaine and Sue and Jeannette to the party as well. When she got to the party, she saw that they had already arrived, looking conspicuously out of place, and noticed Elaine off in a corner with some man. She looked around, disappointed not to see Saul. He wasn't there.

She walked over to Jean. "It's a great party. Is Saul Kaplan coming?"

Jean smiled. "He asked about *you*. He's in the kitchen, which means behind the curtain." Erica smiled and went behind the curtain. She drew it aside and looked in. Saul was leaning against the sink.

"Hi," she said.

"Hi. Looking for me?" he asked teasingly.

"Actually I was," she said. "How's the party?"

"The usual," he said. "Whenever you put about fifty artists into one room you get gossip, paranoia, envy, fear, trembling, hatred, lust, and pretense. It's wonderful."

Erica poured herself some wine and said, "Well,

some of it must be interesting. Tell me something with hatred, lust, and pretense."

"O.K.," he said. "See the one with his arm around Lady Macbeth? His name is Conrad Zweiback, an intense Hungarian. Ambitious, and no talent. The woman is the wife of Henry Gebhart, the critic, a seventy-year-old spider who sets traps for young artists. The wife is the bait."

"Is Gebhart a homosexual?"

"No," Saul said. "Nothing as logical as that. He watches. If Gebhart likes how the young artist performs with Lady Macbeth, he becomes the new discovery."

"How do you know all this?" Erica asked.

"I was discovered by Henry Gebhart," Saul said, laughing. "You look good," he went on. "Do you want to dance?"

"All right."

"Remember," he said, taking her hand, "we really don't know each other."

As they walked to the other end of the loft, Elaine, arm in arm with Charlie, was heading right for them. Erica could see Charlie was very drunk and smoking a joint. He waved to her, pulling Elaine with him.

"Hi, baby," he said to Erica.

"Do you know each other?" Elaine said devilishly. Erica could have killed her. "Charlie tells me he's a great artist," Elaine said.

"Elaine, this is Saul," Erica said.

"What am I?" Charlie snarled. "Chopped liver?"

"Saul Kaplan, Charlie."

"*The* Saul Kaplan," Charlie said, his voice suddenly loud. "Oh, boy, this is a real honor. I bow at your feet, man." And Charlie got on his knees.

Erica wanted to get away. "You're drunk, Charlie," she said.

"And stoned," he said, reeling, trying to get to his feet.

"Is he dangerous?" Elaine said, giggling.

"No, I'm not dangerous, but I'm good. Ask Erica how good I am," he said.

"Shut up, Charlie," Erica said. "Come on, Saul."

Erica started to move away, but Charlie was yelling. "We really got it on one night. Dynamite. We really were into it, and then she goes and shuts the door on me. I mean, what did I do to deserve such a rotten fate? I balled my ass off, and the lady won't see me again."

Erica turned and threw her wine into Charlie's face.

Saul stepped forward. "I think you should go home, Charlie."

Charlie turned to him. "Go fuck off."

"I'll wipe the floor with you." Saul grabbed Charlie's arm.

Erica moved forward. "Saul, let's leave."

"No!" Saul was angry. "He leaves. We stay."

"Oh, I get it," Charlie said, "you're balling her, too."

Saul picked up Charlie by the lapels of his jacket. "Mind your dumb goddamn manners, do you hear?" And then Saul shoved him across the floor, and Charlie, drunk, collapsed against a wall.

Elaine ran over to him, shaking him. "Charlie, are you all right?"

Sue came up behind Erica. "Jesus, are you all right?"

Erica nodded awkwardly and looked across the room. Charlie was standing up now, and Elaine was walking with him toward the door. He was holding his head. Erica felt sick.

When Saul took her hand to take her out for a walk she didn't argue. They walked all over SoHo for almost two hours, talking, being quiet for long stretches, and then a burst of talk again. Finally Saul said, "I think it's time for an egg cream," and pulled her toward a small stand the owner was just closing.

"Why do they call it egg cream?" Erica asked. "No eggs and no cream?"

"Jewish logic," Saul said and shrugged.

They made love that night, and in between talked about marriage and loves and lovers, and Erica knew she was hopelessly falling in love with him.

She knew it for certain when on Saturday she told Patti she thought it would be a good time for her to go to California to see her grandmother. Patti was elated, and Erica felt slightly guilty because she had really agreed because she wanted the time to be with Saul. He had said to her, "Will you ever stay the whole night with me?" and she wanted to, very much. She could have stayed overnight, of course, with Patti still here, but it was the wrong way to handle it and she knew it.

"So are you in love?" Elaine asked.

"Oh, I don't know," Erica said.

"Sounds like you are."

"Well, I like him."

"And Patti's away. Has she met him yet?"

"No."

"Will she?"

"I guess so, eventually. Look, he makes me happy."

"Are you going to get married?"

"God, no."

"That sounds a little final," Elaine said. "I mean, you're going to get married sometime, aren't you?"

"I don't know," Erica said thoughtfully.

"You mean you're swearing off after one bummer? You should at least have two bummers," Elaine said.

"I mean, I just feel different, you know, after all the horror and everything. I mean, I really feel good, different, better, freer. I mean, with all the financial worries and all the junk, I like it better this way."

"That'll change."

"Do you think so, really?"

"Well," Elaine said thoughtfully, "I don't know with you. I mean, you're having this really deep personal blossoming, and I mean, none of us likes to think marriage is a threat to that, but on the other hand, the fact of the matter is it usually is."

"Then why do you want to get married again?"

"Well, I want to more than you. I want to be safe. You'd rather be interesting."

Erica laughed and hung up. Elaine certainly got right to the point. She knew Saul was really interested in her, and she supposed partly she wanted these two weeks to see how things would really go between them. She would spend a lot of time with him, she knew. And it wasn't scaring her.

She had turned to him one morning and, smiling, said, "I don't know why I'm sleeping with you, really. I like it. But I don't want to think about it."

"Lord knows, the last thing in the world I want is you thinking," he'd said, and grabbed her.

She felt happy these days. She slept with him some nights, and some nights came home. She missed him when she did come home, but she felt if she didn't have her own time, that famous word *space*, to herself, she would be unhappy. He cared about her a lot, she knew, and sometimes this worried her because she didn't know finally how important he was to her. She liked being with him. She felt good being with him, and he gave her a lot of rope. He was the most unpossessive, undemanding man she had ever met. Of course, when she told him this, he smiled and said, "It's all a lie. I'm possessive as hell. I'm just controlling myself." But she didn't know, really, whether he was or he was kidding. He seemed to know what she needed; he wasn't simply indulging her, and somehow that made everything much simpler.

And she loved his work. She respected his concern for his work. He had been amazed one day when he had asked her what Martin did and she really had been so hard put to tell him. "He's a stockbroker, that's all I know," she had said, and when he pressed her she realized she really had no idea of what Martin's work was. She knew what he worried about, but she had never really felt any curiosity about what it expressed. She realized that in a fundamental way she had never really been interested in Martin, or perhaps it was that Martin wasn't interested in himself. Saul asked her if she ever thought about him, and she said yes, of course, a lot.

"Now?" he asked.

And she thought, "Well, you know, we did have good times together. It wasn't a nightmare or anything close to that. It was like living in a B-plus situation. I mean, it was fine, you know, but then after he left, it went from F to A-plus, and I had never had A-plus before, you know, and it felt good. I mean, it wasn't Martin's fault. We just slipped into each other somehow. We didn't maintain our independence, and Martin needed something I couldn't or wouldn't give him."

"You said he wanted to be adored."

"He did. But only because I was withdrawn so much. In a funny way I was withdrawn a lot, and he got scareder and scareder. I mean, he needs that girl to make a fuss. Somehow that adoration works to keep him Martin and her Marcia. With us, we coupled ourselves to death. Erica and Martin, Martin and Erica. All that perfect-couple PR didn't help, either."

"Is it totally finished—I mean, you really know? That's a lot of years," Saul said.

"It's really finished," Erica said, knowing fully it was. She was sad about it; she cared about Martin still. But it was like another time, another place.

It was a bizarre coincidence, Erica thought, that the day after she had that conversation with Saul, Martin called to say he had to see her. It was urgent.

"Look," Erica said, "I still go jogging in the morning sometimes. Do you?"

"Yeah," he said. "I'll meet you at Ninety-first Street." And she agreed.

She was surprised to see he wasn't wearing a jogging suit.

"How come?" she asked. "It must be important."

"It is," he said. "I have an appointment, but I thought I'd better see you. How's your money?"

"My money? Well, it's better."

"How's Patti?"

"Fine. You just talked to her yesterday. You must know she's fine."

"Yeah. Well, she said she'd like me to come to the house sometime."

"I told her I could handle that. You can come anytime. Just call first."

"She said you've got a boyfriend."

Erica smiled. "Yes."

Martin took a deep breath. "Marcia and I broke up."

Erica was surprised and said so.

"Yeah," Martin said. "Her friends were half my age. I felt like everyone's father."

"I'm sorry."

"Are you really?"

"Yes. I'm sorry for you."

"Erica"—he reached out and touched her arm; it felt strange—"I want to come back."

"My God"—she looked at him—"how can you even say that?"

"I still love you."

She stood for a moment, the wind sounding very loud in her ears. She couldn't believe it. Her heart was pounding, with what emotion she couldn't be sure.

"No," she said quietly.

"Think of me as someone who had a long illness and recovered."

"It doesn't work, Martin. Over is over."

"How can seventeen years be over in a few months?"

"It is, that's all."

Martin's voice began to sound desperate. "I couldn't help myself. Can you understand that? She made me feel important . . . we could make it better, Erica. I know we could if you'd just try." He reached forward then impulsively and kissed her.

She had to keep herself from shoving him away. Instead, she said quietly, "Martin, I'm sorry. For some people, over is never over. For me, it's really over. I'm not the same. You're not the same."

"Because you found somebody else?" he said piteously.

It stung her to have him ask her like that.

She nodded. "But that's not why, Martin."

He looked at her again, his face turning pale. "I hurt you too much to be forgiven, is that it?"

She looked at him. "I don't know why, Martin. I just know *that*. I couldn't." His face seemed to wince when she said that.

"Why *not*?" he said again. He seemed to implore her. "Erica, please, think about it?"

"I've thought, Martin. No point carrying on about our illusions. What we had was good, but being alone, for me"—she took a deep breath—"what with all the junk, and all of that, it's better."

"Being alone isn't better," he said quietly. "But you're not alone."

"I guess you're right," she said, "but I'm not married, either."

"You want to get divorced and live together?" he asked, his face in a rueful smile.

"With you I'd always be married," she said.

"Was that so bad?" he asked softly.

"It wasn't that it was so bad," she said, tears in her eyes as she looked at him feeling such sadness now. "I just don't want it anymore."

"Good-bye, Erica," he said, and he turned and walked away from her, she thought, very strangely, very slowly.

As Erica watched him walk away, he looked very old, very tired, to her. Something wrenched at her so strongly she nearly ran after him. She pitied him. She never thought she would feel that for Martin. He had always been such a fabulous success to her. What had he done that was so awful? He had left her; that was it. That was so awful she couldn't ever forgive him? No, she never could forgive him. It lay like a pain so deep, and somewhere so familiar, that special kind of hurt, a kind of rejection that nothing could quite displace. She couldn't forgive him. Whatever it was in people that made them forgive, she didn't have it. The humiliation, the rage, the pain had settled into her in some way she didn't like but she had to recognize. Some hard surface had formed, or perhaps it had always been there but only recently come to the top. Trust, whatever its basis, had been broken in a way that couldn't be repaired. Over was over. She had known it the day he told her; she had known it the day she went to bed with Charlie; she had known it when she started falling in love with Saul; she had known it at the restaurant. Whoever Martin had been to her, whatever Martin had been to her, was now gone. "That is why, Martin," she said softly, watching his barely visible figure disappear down the block, "we cannot have it again. It isn't there." She started to jog, which was a relief because from somewhere months of terrible sadness had welled up in her eyes, and tears cascaded down her face in a shuddering, shaking, uncontrollable sense of loss. Along with the anger, the rage, the hurt, there was this final sense of loss. Loss. No more. Martin and Erica were gone. She ran as hard, as fast as she could, trying to outrun the ache that overwhelmed her body, an ache that wrenched her and wracked in a way more profound than anything she had ever known. She had run, she thought, almost two miles when she collapsed in the grass. Heart pounding, eyes tearing, the sobs were still heaving in her chest. Weak with fatigue, she got up and pressed on in a desperate running struggle to convert all the feeling to muscle and bone, to defy the omnipotence of the region called her heart.

When Saul called Erica and told her he wanted to see her, she found herself saying she just had to be alone for a few days. He seemed concerned, and she felt she had been a little sharp, but she felt that after that meeting with Martin, Saul was suddenly, in that context, some kind of intruder. She resented him suddenly, and he knew it.

"Call me when you're ready," he said, somewhat curtly, and hung up.

When she saw Tanya, Erica was composed but puzzled.

"What it is, I think, is that it was one thing for me to be the wronged one, but you know, *he* left *me*. There's a kind of odd liberation in that. I mean, I never felt guilty, I just felt hurt. And then, then that day in the park"—her lip began to quiver—"I felt—oh, God, I can't believe I'm going to cry again." Tanya said nothing, her face looked sad. "I—I just felt like I was sending him away when he needed me, and you know, even with all the horrible stuff, I mean, I felt he needed me, and—and—" Erica broke down again into uncontrollable sobs.

When she was calmer, Tanya said, "You felt he needed you and that was why you couldn't take him back, is that what you feel?"

Erica nodded. "I mean, that's horrible, isn't it? I mean, it's like a drowning man clutching at me and I'm not saving him."

"I think," Tanya said slowly, "you think you would go down with him."

Erica was very quiet. "Which means quite simply that when push comes to shove, I save myself."

"You are human," Tanya said. "You are not God."

Erica nodded. "It's still not cheerful. I mean, what about people who save their children, who give up their lives for their children, men who push their wives into lifeboats?"

"That is different. To you it seems it is a last-minute struggle for air, to stay on the surface. You seem to feel Martin's need would submerge you, drown you. It is need that terrified you, his need for dependency."

"He never had that before," Erica said, her voice quavering. "I couldn't bear to see him so weak"—she was whispering—"I just couldn't take it, I felt such pity. It's such a crummy feeling, pity, and I was overwhelmed with it."

"As if you thought Martin were a baby—that is how you talk about it," Tanya said.

"That's what I kept thinking," Erica said, surprised, "that entire time in the park I kept thinking, 'No one will love him, no one will take care of him, he'll die without me,' like he was a baby, an infant. And you know"—she stared at Tanya—"it's crazy, but I still feel that."

"Do you think you began to feel that toward the end—that summer you withdrew, as you put it, you felt yourself pulling away, the tears, the going to the doctor, all of that?"

Erica nodded. "You know, I never thought about it, but he—just before that summer, he had this business crisis. He lost a lot of money, but that wasn't the worst of it. He got conned." She stared into space. "I never thought he could get conned, but the worst of it was he didn't seem to know what to do. I mean, he wasn't angry, he wasn't anything. He just seemed lost. Lost."

"And what did you do?"

"I turned away from it. I held back. I held him off. I went through the motions because I couldn't really face what was happening to him."

"He was getting weak, you thought?"

"Not I thought. He was. He was lost."

"A man can be strong and still get lost."

"Not to me, he can't," Erica snapped, surprised at that hard edge in her voice.

"You act like being lost is some kind of betrayal," Tanya said gently.

"I hate it. I hated it. I still hate it. I hate seeing him like that," Erica said, hearing the rage in her voice for the first time. "It brings out the worst in me. It makes me run and hide. God," she said, "does this mean I can only make links with men who are King Kong?"

"When you talk about Saul, you talk about strength."

"Yes. He has it."

"There will be times when he may not," Tanya said.

"And then what? Do I bolt and run, is that what you're saying? Any crack in the surface and I'm on the run? Is that what I *am*? God," Erica said quietly in Tanya's office, wondering what kind of a wretch she was. "That's what it was with Charlie, of course, part of it. I mean, in bed he was king, daylight he got vulnerable. I couldn't stand it."

Tanya said nothing. Erica sat for what seemed a long while and stared into space. She was beginning, she thought, to put it together.

Erica spent the next three days alone, utterly alone. She really didn't know what she was doing, but she was essentially putting her house in order—literally—dusting and reorganizing and in between working on her painting. She felt she was thinking, coming to grips. Something. Whatever all the horror had been with Martin the last few months, she felt finally something good was coming out of it. And she was glad Patti had been away. Patti did not need to see her mother in the kind of state Erica had been in, and Erica felt that if Patti had been there, she would have held back in some way. She would be glad to see her, though. She missed her.

17

Erica thought that perhaps there was nothing more wonderful than a grandmother when she saw how happy Patti looked when she came back from California.

"How was it?" she asked, kissing her.

"It was great, Mom," Patti said. "There's nothing like two weeks, twenty-four hours a day, of coddling, pampering, and unconditional love."

"That's what grandmothers are for," Erica said, hugging her, very glad to see her.

"What's up with you?" Patti asked. "You been seeing that guy?"

"What guy?"

"You know, Saul."

"Yes, I've been seeing him," Erica said, as they walked to the baggage terminal.

"You like him?" She heard a lot in the question.

"I like him," Erica said, "and he wants to meet you."

"I might not like him," Patti said.

"You might not," Erica said, looking at her, "but I'd like you to try."

"Oh-oh," Patti said, "sounds serious. When do I meet him?"

"For dinner, tomorrow night."

"O.K.," Patti said, "because tonight I have to see Phil."

And Erica burst out laughing. She had orchestrated everything so she would have time to spend tonight with Patti and only with Patti, and Patti wanted to see Phil. She had had all she could do to keep him from joining her at the airport. "Look, Phil," she had said, "when you're married, you'll meet her at the airport, but you're not married."

"You're very possessive, Mrs. Benton," he had said, "but I understand." Smart-ass kid. There were times when she wanted to slug him.

When Erica had called Saul to invite him to dinner, he had said, "Look, Erica, you've got to make up your mind. Either you're going to spend time with me or you're not. I can't take any more of these weekend freeze-outs."

"What do you mean?" She was surprised.

"I mean, you can't see me, you can't talk to me on the phone even, you have to be alone. I mean, what is that?"

"Saul, I'm not seeing anyone else. I—I—Martin saw me again. He asked me to take him back."

"And you needed time to think it over?" His voice was bitter.

"No. I didn't need time to think it over. I told him no. It just brought a lot out. I'm sorry. I told you I need a lot of space now. Don't push me."

To her surprise, he relented. "O.K.," he said softly, "I've been through it. I ought to know. It's hard to be on this end, though." There was a pause. "What time do you want me for dinner?"

By the time it was time for Saul to arrive, Erica felt as if she were a teenager introducing her prom date to her mother. Patti kept asking a million questions. "Is he handsome, is he tall, are you in love with him, are you going to marry him, how good an artist is he, I don't think I'm going to like him, I saw Daddy, he looked terrible, his girl friend left him, he said you won't take him back, I said you were too mad but maybe someday you would." That last had gotten Erica, but only temporarily. She breezed past it, somehow, and was relieved finally when Saul was at the door.

The first thing Patti said to Saul was, "I've seen one of your paintings at the Museum of Modern Art."

"Did you like it?" Saul asked.

"I didn't understand it," Patti said.

"She never lies," Erica said quickly.

Then Patti asked, "How old are you?"

Saul stared at her. "I'm forty-two."

"You don't look it," Patti said.

"Ah," Saul said, on guard.

"You look older," she said.

"Patti," Erica said, "don't be hostile."

"I wasn't being hostile. . . . How old do I look?"

Saul smiled and looked at her carefully. "It's hard to tell with young women. . . . I already know you're fifteen."

"Yeah, but do I look it?" Patti said—almost preening, Erica thought.

"You look older," Saul said. Patti smiled and turned away.

When Erica poured the wine, she asked to have some. She never did, so Erica hesitated until Saul said, "Cut it with water, like the French do."

"We're not French," Erica protested.

"Booze is worse for you than grass," Patti said smugly.

"Cut it out, Patti." Erica was getting irritated.

"I smoke grass," Patti said.

"So do I," Saul said slowly.

"Patti, you're too precocious," Erica said. "I don't like you smoking grass. I've told you. Several times."

"I know. But I'm not precocious. I'm just normal.

As a matter of fact, I'm not even normal. I'm still a virgin."

"Shut up, Patti," Erica snapped.

"Fifteen is a difficult age," Saul said almost sympathetically.

"So is thirty-six," Erica snapped again. "Let's eat."

In the kitchen, Erica told Patti she was being rude.

"I'm nervous, Mom," she said. "You never brought a man home before."

"Well, do you like him?" Erica asked.

"It's too early to tell," Patti said.

"Your mother is a great cook," Saul said when Erica sat down.

"How do you know from one dish?" Patti said resentfully.

"Oh," he said, "she made eggs for me one night."

"With hot sauce and grated cheese?"

"Yeah."

"She really likes you, then."

"I'm not having fun," Erica said wryly.

"I am." Saul reached over and touched her arm.

"Relax, Mom. I know you and Saul are lovers."

Saul burst out laughing, but Erica was angry. "That's not funny. You're being hostile, Patti, and I don't like it."

"Well, you're the one who's being hostile. You always told me to tell the truth. Obviously you invited Saul here to prepare me, so you're not telling the truth." The outburst surprised Erica.

"Patti, I invited myself here. I wanted to meet you," Saul said quietly.

"I have a father. I don't need another one," Patti said harshly.

"I don't want to be your father," Saul said.

Patti sat for a moment, her face red. Suddenly she got up and left the table.

"Well," Erica said, "life is full of surprises."

"She'll get over it," Saul said.

"You're a threat to her," Erica said.

He looked at her. "Go talk to her. I'll wait." And Erica left the room.

She was annoyed at Patti for behaving like a fifteen-year-old, and she knew it. She walked into Patti's room, where the radio was blasting and Patti was sulking in a corner.

"I know what you're going to say," Patti said. "I'm acting awful. I know I am. I'm sorry."

"What's the matter?"

"I can't get used to it."

"I'm not marrying Saul, Patti."

"You can marry him."

"No one is asking you to stop loving your father."

Patti began to cry, and then quickly stopped. "I know," she sniffed. "I'm sorry."

When Patti and Erica returned to the room, Patti said brightly, "How'd you get to be an abstract expressionist?"

"Well, I'll tell you," Saul said, leaning back. "I was born in London, you know. My father owned a delicatessen in Stepney Green—that's the Lower East Side of London. One day when I was six, my parents had an argument. My mother threw a pickled herring at Dad—it missed him but splattered against the wall—I thought it was gorgeous. That's when I became an abstract expressionist."

Patti laughed. "I bet it's probably true."

"Why?" he asked. "Does my work remind you of a pickled herring?"

"Yes," she said thoughtfully. "A splattered pickled herring."

They laughed, the mood shifted, and Erica felt relieved. Not so great, but not so bad, either.

18

WHEN THE TIME CAME for Erica's formal divorce papers to be filed, she told Martin she had decided she wanted to sell the house. They would split the proceeds, and she would then ask only for support for Patti. He thought she was trying to do him a favor, which embarrassed her to the point where she said, "I'm doing it for myself, Martin. I want to be free of as many entanglements as I can."

It also gave her an excuse to work up her nerve to ask Herb for a raise again. After an anticipated protest on his part, she agreed to work two nights a week and got him to agree to close to what she wanted. She was aware that Saul was vaguely disapproving of her drive toward financial independence. "Erica," he had said to her, "look, I have plenty of money. Why are you so worried about it?"

"Saul," she said quietly, "I'm crazy about you. You know that, but I don't want anybody to support me."

"If you had it," he said, "I'd take it."

"You're an artist," she said, smiling. And he laughed.

When Erica told Elaine she had definitely decided to sell the house, Elaine got all excited. She turned out to be a trooper of an apartment looker, and inside of three weeks Erica had found the apartment she wanted. To her surprise, Patti seemed eager to move, too.

"Well, it's definitely not the Upper East Side," Elaine

said when she came to inspect it. "But it's got good light. And it's not depressing. Why are you giving Patti such a big room, though?"

"Because she needs more space. Also, that guy Phil practically lives here."

"Who's that? The boyfriend?"

"Yeah, the boyfriend, but no sex."

"That's what they all say," Elaine said smugly. "I'll tell you it's small, but it's cheery. Can you afford it?"

"Yeah, with the money from the house and child support, I can afford it. I don't want to use all the house money. I'm thinking maybe someday of opening a small gallery. I spoke to Herb, and, well, maybe. . . ."

"Then take," Elaine said softly. "Wow, opening a gallery. You never told me that."

"Well," Erica said, "I don't know, of course. But you know, Herb likes the idea, and I will have the money, and there is room for it. I mean, it's exciting, isn't it?" She *was* excited. She could see Elaine was jealous.

"What's the matter?" Erica said.

"I can't stand it."

"What can't you stand?"

"The way things work out for you."

"What do you mean?"

"Well, when Sue hears you're opening a gallery, she'll die. That's all. You just have things work out for you. I don't know," Elaine said, looking depressed. "They don't work out for me. Hey, Erica, that guy Charlie, did he ever say anything about me?"

Erica turned. "Are you really interested?"

Elaine shrugged. "Well, I thought he really liked me. I was surprised he never called."

"Well"—Erica smiled—"actually he did say something."

"What?"

"He came into the gallery to apologize for that night, and he said he really always went for women who left him and it was his fault. He was very nice."

"I don't care if he was nice. What did he say about me?"

Erica could hardly suppress a giggle. "He said he liked you, and you would be good for him because you'd never leave him, but the idea scared him."

"What on earth? What balls, what nerve. Where'd he get the idea I'd never leave him?" Elaine was storming around the living room in an outraged huff.

Erica suddenly burst into laughter. "Oh, Elaine, he said you'd never leave him because—because"—she could hardly get it out—"you're boy-crazy!" Elaine stopped pacing and grinned, and then broke into peals of laughter.

"Boy-crazy! That's hysterical," she roared, and collapsed back against the living-room wall. "Boy-crazy! Oh, my God." Tears were streaming down their cheeks, the two of them were laughing so hard. "I spent—I spent"—Elaine could hardly draw a breath—"two years at the shrink's, and all along he could have told me my"—she gasped—"my problem. I'm boy-crazy!" She screamed this last out, and Erica rolled over, grabbing her stomach, her sides aching from the hysterical laughter that washed over them. Boy-crazy; it was hysterically funny because it was true.

Patti came in in a few minutes and found her mother and Elaine rolling on the floor in hysterics. She broke into smiles. "Hey, if this is the vibes in the new place, I like it, but what's so funny?" Phil was standing beside her.

"Oh, nothing," Erica said, wiping her eyes. "Elaine just found out, she just had a revelation."

"What's that?" Patti asked.

"I'm boy-crazy," Elaine said, bursting into hysterics

again, and Patti and Phil just stood there looking dumbfounded and vaguely disapproving.

"Come on, Phil. They're crazy, period." And Patti took him to explore the rest of the apartment. Erica could hear her yelling, "Hey, it's not as bad as it looked at night. It looks good in the daytime, don't you think?"

19

ERICA KNEW THAT SAUL was hoping she would not take the apartment. He was going to Vermont for the summer, and he wanted her there with him, so she was surprised when he sounded so pleased she'd made the decision.

"I thought you'd be mad," she said.

"I was. But I gave up. You're determined to be tough, independent, sexy, beautiful, and irresistible. I'm coming over."

"Meet me at the new place, I want you to see it."

So he did. When he drove up, he was hauling a huge canvas out of the car, and Erica ran out to meet him.

"What's this?"

"A housewarming present."

"Saul! Let me see it!" She tore the wrapping from the canvas in the street. It was one of her favorites.

"Oh, Saul!" She was ecstatic he had given it to her. "But I can't! Saul! It's so valuable."

"I'm giving it to you for purely selfish reasons."

"What?"

"Every time you're even thinking about anybody else, it will be right there staring at you. A guilt totem."

She laughed and helped him carry it inside. It was wonderful.

"Saul," she said to him later, "do you understand why I can't spend the summer with you?"

"Yes and no."

"Well, for one thing, I couldn't get the time. Herb just gave me a big raise. And we have plans."

"What's the other thing?"

"Well, what would I do up there all summer? Watch you paint? Pick berries? I'd go nuts."

"You'd be with me. We'd spend time together. It's not so hard to do nothing but have a good time for a few months."

"Saul," Erica said quietly, "I was on vacation for seventeen years. For me it's hard."

"Do you know what it's like up there in the woods, all alone? I'm going to go crazy."

"Paint."

"That's not enough."

"Am I only a sex object?" she asked.

"No, you're a willful, stubborn, curious woman who is also a sex object."

"Why don't you come back every weekend?"

"Because I'm a creature of routine. When I start to paint, I can't stop. Come with me, for chrissake!" He moved toward her. "Come on," he said, his voice changing, "you know you will."

"Saul!" Erica couldn't believe he was serious. And then she saw he was. "Saul, I just signed the lease—you said you understood."

"I'll pay for your rent, you can come back, come on Erica, I mean for chrissake I'm not going to spend the whole damn summer alone." He beat his fist into the wall and Erica was flabbergasted to see he was so angry.

Suddenly she felt hot, hot with fury. "You were *humoring* me!" She was screaming at him. "You expected me to come, what nerve, Saul! Why? *Because* you wanted me to, that's why."

"That's reason enough for me," he said quickly.

They had paired off and were facing each other glaring now.

"Well it's not for me!" Erica was fuming, "I've been

doing what one man wants for seventeen years and I'm not about to start the habit with someone else." Saul was looking at her with total disgust. She was absolutely amazed.

"Erica," he said finally, impatiently, "living with me doesn't mean doing only what *I* want."

"Like hell it doesn't," she said, more bitterly than she intended.

It seemed like a long time before Saul said, "So you're not coming with me."

"No."

"And you're never going to live with me?"

"No." She paused. Then she was quiet. "Not for a long time, Saul."

"I had it figured wrong."

She felt sick. He sounded so hurt. Yet she hated him for trying to make her go, for making her want to go, for making her feel that old tear, to be oneself, to be with someone else.

"Saul, it doesn't mean I don't love you." It was difficult for her to say it, and she said it with sadness, and rage. Then more quietly "Saul, don't make me feel I'm deserting you. If I go, I'm deserting me."

He sighed, and looked up, nodding slowly, trying to understand.

"I'm sorry," she said, trembling, "I can't, I just can't."

"Come here, I want to give you something to remember me by." He reached for her, but she pulled away. "You're too tough," he said.

"I'm just honest," she protested, giving in to him.

"Actually," he said, kissing her, "fortunately, you're not *that* tough."

"Hey," Erica said, "what's more important to you, my body or my heart?"

"At the moment," he said, caressing her, "I'm afraid I'll sound crass."

She laughed and collapsed against him, this man who

made her happy, who made her feel good in so many ways she could hardly believe it was true. As they made love, she knew she would miss him terribly, that she would have to miss him, yet she wouldn't go.

"I'll come up for Memorial Day," she said as they walked to his car. "I'd like to meet your kids."

"Sometimes they're awful," he said.

"Sometimes *I'm* awful," she said.

"I've noticed," he said teasingly. Then he turned on the street to look at her. "Erica, you're a tough case. There's an awful lot of independence there for one man to handle."

She smiled. "You do better than handle it," she said.

He turned to her and touched her face. "You betcha," he said softly, "and you haven't seen anything yet."